# The Case of
# The Babbling
# SPHINX

## by Bob Nailor

Paperback: ISBN: 978-1-61877-172-8

Ebook: ISBN: 978-1-61877-173-5

# The Case of

# The Babbling Sphinx

Discover other titles by Bob Nailor at

www.bobnailor.com

Cover by Bob Nailor

Table of Contents

# CHAPTER ONE ~ The Mansion

"May I help you?" the gate's squawk box grated into life.

"Detective Barry Hargrove to see Amelia Eggers."

"Do you have an appointment?"

"Not really," I said. "When I spoke with her this morning, she said she'd notify... ah, the name is..." I struggled through my notes. "Uh... yes, Aswad. She was going to notify Aswad of my arrival."

"One minute, please."

I looked at my old Bulova and watched the timepiece click off the seconds. Twenty-two seconds.

"The gates will open Detective Hargrove. Drive the main road to the house and park beside the statue of Osiris with the smaller statue of Anubis at his feet." There was a pause. "You do know who and what Osiris and Anubis are?"

*Osiris? Anubis?* The thought was a question. *Sure I knew who Osiris and Anubis were; Egyptian gods.* I rolled a shoulder and waited for the large steel gate to glide to one side.

During the quarter-mile drive I noticed the mansion, to the west of the mansion, a large glass structure, and something in a sandstone color. I attempted to glance between the trees and shrubs for a better view. The tree and bush-lined driveway opened and the mansion stood in its full glory. I parked under the blank stare of twenty-foot-tall Osiris, god of birth and death. At his feet, a six-foot statue of Anubis stood guard.

I strolled on the large inlay of stones creating the majestic entryway before the main door of the mansion. The residence reminded me of an Egyptian temple. I took a moment to take in the vista. I frowned. The pond's Oriental decor confused me. A large circular driveway enclosed a huge pool of crystal-clear water. A fountain sprayed upward and a beautiful pagoda stood in the middle of an island within the pool.

I watched it for a moment, seeing the intricate painted tiles glisten in the sunlight.

*That can't be gold*, I thought. Yet, it didn't appear to be otherwise. I glanced back at the ebony statue of Anubis. *Onyx*, I thought. I shook my head. It had to be since it didn't appear to be a black painted statue. There was no doubt in my mind that Osiris was marble. I inhaled deeply, taking in the scents. *Obviously, no expense was too much*, I thought.

The door glided open as I approached.

"Welcome, Detective Hargrove. My name is Aswad. Mrs. Eggers is in her library. Please, follow me."

*Her library?* I thought. *Usually it is just the library.* I grinned at the idea. *A his and her library.*

He closed the door behind me, stepped around, and proceeded across the grand foyer with the dual staircases leading to the upper level. A ten-foot-wide crystal chandelier draped from above. A glass dome above allowed for the sunlight to glisten, sparkle and diffuse throughout the foyer. A million rainbows floated everywhere.

The butler opened a set of double doors and motioned for me to enter. I felt a slight breeze as the doors closed behind when I entered the library. The doors clicked shut.

Amelia stood by a desk, her hands holding an open scroll. I surveyed the room. Books, more books, and hundreds of scrolls cluttered the myriad shelves. She had changed into a different outfit. Gone was the morning frock consisting of a silver lamé evening gown with a sparkling rhinestone top. Instead she now wore a simple kalasiris, a simple linen tube dress, cinched at the waist with a jewel encrusted belt.

I ambled to the desk, taking the time for me to purvey the scrolls Amelia had stretched across it.

"Do you read hieroglyphics?" she asked, noticing my glancing at the scrolls.

"I'm familiar with a few of the symbols," I replied and pointed. "This is Ra." I cocked my head. "And this one is Cleopatra VII. Interesting." I smiled. "The last pharaoh of Egypt."

"You amaze me, Detective Hargrove," Amelia moved to glance at the symbols. "You're quite correct."

"Such a pity Cleopatra died at such a young age. Viper's bite." I leaned to open another scroll, one that appeared quite new.

"If you don't mind," Amelia said. "Please don't touch them with your hands." She removed her gloves. "The human oils can damage such artifacts as these."

"My apologies," I offered. "I thought these to be copies. I didn't realize they—" I stopped and leaned in for a closer look. "This is genuine papyrus."

"Yes, Detective Hargrove," Amelia said. "Mr. Eggers allows me several luxuries. I travel to Egypt and send home these artifacts.

I considered her words. Artifacts? Something told me these were stolen goods, rustled from a tomb. I surveyed the room, this time with my interest on the scrolls. My mind staggered at the number of them as I studied the shelves, counting silently as I estimated how many. Over three hundred.

"What do your books contain?" I asked and pointed randomly at different books on the shelves.

"Various subjects," she replied. "Some history. Some art. Some... shall I say, for the most part, the books are esoteric except to the more discerning types. My heritage lives in me. I am one of the few Egyptians who can prove the purity of their lineage."

I nodded. *Impressive*, I thought.

"Now, if you could show me a few things." I took out my notepad. "I would like to see where you last saw your husband." I hesitated. "The balcony as you called it? Also, his bedroom and the sun room. I will want to spend the most time in those locations, but I still wish to see the other rooms and if you don't mind, I will wander the estate grounds."

"This way, detective," Amelia said. "We will go upstairs to see his bedroom, my bedroom, and the other rooms on that floor.

"You mentioned a nurse. I was wondering—"

"She will be sitting in his bedroom. Her name is Susan

Williams."

I frowned, unsure why the nurse would be in Mr. Eggers room.

Amelia opened a door. "This is my husband's bedroom."

A young woman dressed in a freshly pressed white uniform stood as I entered.

"May I introduce, Miss Susan Williams, his attending nurse." Amelia turned to me. "This is Detective Hargrove."

I strode over to her, my notepad in hand.

"Glad to meet you, Miss Williams. Now, as I understand, you were the last person to see Mr. Eggers? Is that correct?"

The young woman blanched, stepping back.

"I didn't see Mr. Eggers last night," she mumbled. "I came on shift at eight this morning. According to Miss Rines, he didn't come into the bedroom. It was assumed he was in... I mean, he decided to..." She shook her head. "Miss Rines said she was alone all night."

"And this Miss Rines is who?" I held pen to paper, waiting for the answer.

"There are three nurses, Detective Hargrove," Amelia interrupted. "They work twelve hour shifts with twenty-four hours off." She smiled. "The other two nurses are Janet Rines and Kathy Whittaker."

"Fine," I said and scribbled a note in my pad. "May I have your address and phone, Miss Williams?"

"I live here," she said. "As do the other two nurses."

"So, basically you sit here twelve hours, keeping tabs on Mr. Eggers. Is that correct?"

Susan nodded. "We are here in case of an emergency."

"Emergency," I repeated. "Such as?"

"If the electricity were to go off, Mr. Eggers' c-pap machine would stop working and if he is in a sound sleep, he could possibly suffocate."

I turned to Amelia. "Really? A mansion with no backup generator?"

"It turns on within three seconds of power shortage." Susan was quick to answer.

I smiled. "At least, the suffocation aspect is of no concern."

"We are trained, Detective Hargrove, for any emergency including a heart attack." Susan cocked an eye of attitude. "If the power went out, the lack of air flow to Mr. Eggers c-pap mask might be enough to cause him to go into a cardiac arrest. You do realize that mask is his only source of air."

"I am quite familiar with c-pap machines; my father has one. Now, what would you do if he died of natural causes during the night?" I asked.

She gave me a quizzical look. "Natural causes?"

I shrugged. "Mr. Eggers is a gentleman up in his years. At some point, the heart is going to just plain stop."

"We immediately begin resuscitation efforts." She heaved a sigh. "Our job is to keep Mr. Eggers alive as long as possible."

I wrote in my notepad: eternal life - right.

"We all die, Miss Williams," I finally said. "For now, that's the only questions I have." I paused. "Oh, wait. Was Mr. Eggers on any medications?"

"Yes, he had a few." She reached for a sheet of paper on the bedside table. "Here's a list of them." She handed me the list. "Some for his heart, some for his blood pressure, and a few others."

I scanned the list. Nothing seemed out of place. I recognized most of the medications.

"Thank you, Miss Williams," I said and, once more, surveyed the bedroom with its heavy brocade curtains, dark wood paneling, plush carpeting and expensive art work adorning the walls.

Then it caught my eye. A snapshot of the sphinx near the pyramids of Egypt. It was so out of place with the other paintings by the greats: Rembrandt, van Gogh, Monet, da Vinci, Dali, and Picasso.

I pointed at the photo. "Interesting shot," I said.

"On our honeymoon," Amelia offered. "That is us standing in front of Great Sphinx of Giza. Our guide snapped the shot. Gregory loves Egypt."

I frowned. "I thought you said he was a recluse, never leaving the mansion grounds. This is what? Six years ago?"

"The picture was 'doctored' to put him in the image. I went. He stayed here and we had him dressed like that and he was super-imposed in to create a new picture. We have others throughout the mansion. Gregory loves to travel."

*A world traveler who never leaves home*, I thought. "Now, if you don't mind, may I see your room?"

Amelia nodded and I followed.

It was exactly as I imagined it. I noted the emergency button on the nightstand she had told me about. Sheer curtains billowed as the wind entered the room through the huge arched door way to a balcony. I could smell cinnamon and... My mind searched for the scent. It lingered just on the edge of my mind.

Licorice! It was an earthy scent and there was more.

I stared out the doorway to the balcony as the curtains once more wafted into the room. In the distance I could see the pyramidal greenhouse. My mind wandered.

Shaking the cobwebs out of my brain, I returned to my inspection of Amelia's bedroom. Shades of lavender, rouge red, pristine yellow mixed with the black lines. Definitely very Egyptian appearing. She did enjoy her heritage.

I nodded. "Guess I should check out the main floor..." I hesitated. "And where the party was held." I once more gazed out the window. "Oh, and I must go walk the grounds." I smiled at Mrs. Eggers. "Of course, first I want to see where you last saw your husband. If I remember correctly, it was a balcony?" I frowned. "On the first floor?"

She nodded and led me down the magnificent staircase. I watched the rainbows dance about the foyer. It was magical and mesmerizing.

"The party was held here." She opened the doors to a large room. "I understand Gregory's parents had grand parties here when they were alive." She shrugged. "I'm told the parties were the social events of the year."

I nodded my head while taking in the sheer size of the room. It could easily hold over one hundred guests with sufficient room to dance and hold tables laden with foodstuffs.

She strode across the open space. "Gregory was here, speaking to the Chinese dignitaries and then they went out over there." She pointed toward the main doors. "I went to this balcony." She sashayed to the double doors. "It is more of an opening to allow fresh air to circulate in than a true balcony." She shrugged. "Still, it allows me to step from the room. I could see and hear some of what was going on."

"Which was all spoken in Chinese, is that correct?" I asked, remembering what she had told me earlier that day when she hired me.

Again, she nodded. "I don't know who the stranger was, but when things became hostile, Gregory's security men assisted the person to the backseat of the limo." She attempted a feeble smile. "The Chinese dignitaries apologized and bowed many times over as the vehicle drove away."

I watched her.

Amelia heaved a heavy sigh. "That was the last time I saw my husband. I went back to the party." She gazed at me, her eyes widening. "I was the hostess. There were guests, after all. I couldn't just disappear." She shrugged. "Plus, the Chinese dignitaries rejoined the festivities, but Gregory wasn't with them. I figured he was either talking with somebody outside, or he'd escaped to his office.

# CHAPTER TWO ~ The Pyramid

"You've seen our bedrooms, the ballroom, the balcony, the foyer, and several other rooms..." Amelia pursed her lips. "Exactly what would you like to see next?"

"The grounds," I replied. "Especially the pagoda I noticed as I drove up."

"Ah, yes, the pagoda," Amelia repeated. "Gregory was extremely proud of his dual heritage: part Egyptian, part Chinese. He had the pagoda added to honor his mother when she passed."

"Would you like me to get the grounds keeper to assist you?" It was the butler who had quietly approached behind me.

Startled, I recouped my composure. "No need to bother him," I said. "I'll just wander around." I rolled a shoulder. "You know, snooping." I glanced at Amelia. "Unless that is a problem."

"I have nothing to hide," she said. "Wander. Snoop." She grinned. "Just be sure to be off the grounds before sunset when the dogs are released."

I frowned.

"Part of the security." She smiled, yet there was something hiding behind that smile.

My mind raced. *Dogs?* "Tell me, Mrs. Eggers." I turned to face the large front door and pointed. "Were the dogs released the night of the party?" I turned back to face her.

Amelia's eyes widened in shock. "Of course not," she said. "They'd tear the guests to pieces." She placed a hand to her lower throat. "Trust me, any trespasser would be practically unrecognizable if the security guards don't blow the safety whistle to control them." Regaining her composure, she smiled. "The dogs have been well-trained."

The butler guided me to the front door.

"Please ring when you are finished," he said and pointed to an ornate doorbell.

"Will do," I said and sauntered my way across the driveway, passing under the shadowy watch of Osiris. "I will want to see the downstairs," I hollered to the butler as he stood in the open doorway, watching me. "I mean the basement, if there is one."

"Yes, of course," he replied.

I strolled to the large pool with the island pagoda. Again, the structure seemed out of place with all the other Egyptian motif, but I wasn't the owner or designer. I stepped carefully on the cement lily pads leading to the island. The pagoda was cool and refreshing with a breeze gently wafting through the fancy lattice.

Blood. Small. Insignificant. Almost undetectable on the foot of the settee. Yet, it glared at me like a beacon. Suddenly the scent of bleach tickled my nose. There was a discreet smell of cinnamon and citrus attempting to cover the faint hint of bleach.

*Somebody was severely hurt or died here. There has been some intense cleaning here*, I thought and considered taking a sample. *No need to mess with a crime scene. Willie will have my head if I contaminate the area.* I considered sitting to contemplate but realized I might contaminate the scene, so I strolled the inside perimeter of the pagoda, studying the views and meditating. I once more stood in the archway where I'd entered the pagoda. I reviewed. The settee with the blood was positioned so the person sitting would have a clear view of the main entrance and any vehicle coming up the driveway. On the opposite side, the settee allowed a view of the pyramid and with a slight turn, the main door of the mansion. In the middle of the space was a large pillow. *For meditation?* I questioned and frowned. Shaking my head to clear it, I stepped gingerly back the way I'd come and quickly found myself on the driveway.

I closed my eyes to allow everything I'd viewed today saturate my brain so it could process the information.

Amelia claimed it was a missing husband, but I now suspected foul play. Suddenly her words rang loudly in the ears: The wife is always the first suspect. If Gregory is missing, find him; if he is dead; find the murderer. I opened my eyes.

Ahead of me was a large open expanse of green lawn... and the gigantic pyramidal greenhouse. It fascinated me. It was a magnificent, yet a smaller crystal imagining of the Great Pyramid of Giza. Not as large as Khufu's Great Pyramid, it was still much larger than the Louvre Pyramid in Paris. As I walked, the closer I got, the larger I realized the pyramid actually was. The peak had to be near one-hundred-fifty feet at the zenith.

Something caught my eye. A mass of yellow-brown blurred through the lower glass panes of the pyramid. It was large and was on the east side of the pyramid. I nodded, remembering the sandstone item I'd noticed on my entrance onto the mansion property.

Unsure what it was, my footsteps speed up in a haste to discover this anomaly. As I approached, the mass took substance, but was still unfamiliar. As I turned the corner, the structure took existence.

It was a sphinx. One made of what appeared to be stained stucco. I touched the surface. It was not stucco. It was solid rock. I stood back and admired the handy work of the sculptor.

*This had to take...* My mind boggled. I had no idea how many worked on the project nor for how long. Months? Years?

Putting a hand to cover my forehead, I leaned back to look up. The sphinx had to be at least thirty or forty feet high at the top of the head. *Four stories,* I thought. Immediately I gazed at the pyramid behind the sphinx which faced east.

I squinted to see in the bright sunlight. *At least one-hundred fifty feet high,* I thought. *Fifteen floors!*

Inside the pyramid I could see palms, tall palms stretching to touch the slanting edges of the pyramid. A door led into the pyramid. I strolled along the sphinx, allowing my hand to slide against the body of the great creature. It was extremely smooth... then I felt a crevice.

*Huh?* I stopped and inspected the almost hidden crack. My fingers worked the edge. It appeared to be a door, a well-hidden door. *I'll come back to this,* I thought. The nearby pyramid doorway beckoned.

I opened the door of the greenhouse and was immediately assaulted with the humid air within. Scents carried on the air. I attempted to connect the aroma to a name... myrhh, cinnamon, rose, lily, henna, and...

The scent alluded me. I could almost taste it on the air, it was... it was... cardamom. The pyramid was amazing. The size alone was mind-boggling. Palms and exotic trees soared up to the heights of the glass enclosure.

There were rows and rows of lilies. Their heady scent mingled with the other perfumes and I was reminded of a French perfume distillery.

Resin oozed from a tree's incision. I leaned down for a closer inspection. No doubt, it was myrhh. The light golden color and scent assured me I was correct.

"Do you have any questions?"

Startled, I turned to face a gardener who had quietly come up on my blind side.

"No. I'm fine," I replied. "My name is Barry Hargrove, a detective hired by Mrs. Eggers. I was just enjoying the myriad of smells."

He nodded and stuck out a hand to shake. "I'm the head gardener. Jose Mendez. Mrs. Eggers enjoys walking and picking her flowers." He turned to gaze at the door. "Would you like me to show you the grounds and assist you."

I smiled. "Like I told Aswad, I'm fine. I'll just wander and snoop." I laughed.

"Si," he replied, turned, and left me.

I quickly did a simple search of the pyramid and decided my time could be better spent checking the hidden doorway in the sphinx. I headed for the door I'd come in.

The sphinx loomed before me. I worked my way along the side, sliding my hand on the smooth body, hoping to find the crevice I'd discovered earlier.

Nothing. The indentation was gone.

I decided to do a walk-around of the sphinx to see it from all the sides. The front paws stretched out and deep between them, near the chest, a tall tablet stood. Not a tablet. It was an obelisk. I gazed at the hieroglyphics, recognizing a few of the characters. It definitely was not a copy. This was the real thing. I continued my inspection, finally rounding back to the side I'd searched earlier.

A sound caught my attention. The hidden door opened.

I stepped back behind the sphinx and watched as the butler stepped into the sunlight. He stretched up and touched the sphinx. The door closed.

The butler glanced at the pyramid and I immediately stepped back into the shadows of the sphinx's backside, hoping Aswad hadn't seen me. I waited a few seconds before peeking around to see what he was doing.

Aswad wasn't there. I stepped out and scanned the area. There, in the distance, the butler retreated quickly toward the mansion. He carried something.

My eyes immediately began to scan the side of the sphinx. I had to find that door.

I scrutinized the ground, seeing the crushed grass where the butler had stepped out of the sphinx. I immediately turned and stretched up to let my fingers play on the surface, hoping to find a button or toggle to the door.

CLICK.

# CHAPTER THREE ~ The Sphinx

The dark opening begged me to enter. I did a quick check to my left and right. Nobody. I stepped into the entrance.

Immediately, lights clicked on. There was a hallway to my right. I stepped in that direction.

The secret entry door closed.

*At least when I come back, I know the door is right there*, I thought and continued to follow the lighted passageway.

I knew I was headed toward the front of the sphinx and the legs. I questioned the logic of this action.

The passageway turned to my left. I followed. Another twenty steps, again, the passageway turned to the left... and ended.

I faced a wall with hieroglyphics. They were unfamiliar, I didn't recognize any of them.

A soft click sounded. I timed it. One per second. My mind raced to estimate how many I'd heard so far. I counted, trying to add what I thought the number passed could be.

Fifty-six. Fifty-seven. Fifty-eight. Fifty...

The lights turned off. I stood in utter darkness. I waited for my eyes to adjust. They didn't. There was no light. I figured my irises were as full as my eyes could hold, and still, I saw nothing.

A slight scraping sound caught my attention. It was on the floor. Something moved.

I reached in my pocket and retrieved my lighter. A quick movement of my fingers and the lighter burst into flame.

My eyes immediately squinted in the harshness of the bright light of the fire.

Into the shadows something scrambled across the floor and into the wall before me.

*So*, I thought. *There is something behind this wall.*

I stared at the wall and the mysterious symbols. Suddenly, one of them didn't seem to fit. It was an arrow pointing to the left and was on the very left edge of the wall. I moved my hand over the wall of inscriptions hoping to find some type of toggle.

Nothing.

I moved my hand to the wall at the left of the arrow. Again, I played my hand over the surface, searching for...

CLICK.

The wall before me turned on a center balance. A lighted passage awaited on the other side.

*Okay, Barry*, I thought. *Do you move forward or do you turn and go back?*

The answer was obvious, I stepped through the opening into the new passageway.

As I expected, the opening swung closed behind me. Again, I was locked into wherever I was going. The passageway turned to the right. Steps led downward.

I was confused. I had not felt any sensation of moving upwards, so this could only mean I was now moving below the surface of the mansion grounds.

I walked down the stairs. At the landing, the passageway turned left. Expecting another passageway, I was surprised to discover it turned left again and stairs continued down. I was headed back the way I'd come. Searching ahead in the dim light, I could see another landing at the bottom.

Expecting another turn, I was surprised to discover it was a dead-end. I was at the bottom of the stairs with three walls surrounding me.

To my left was Anubis, the Egyptian god of Death. He faced me. In front of me was Osiris, he faced to the right. And, on my right side, was Anubis who faced left.

*This is an interesting turn of events*, I thought as I considered the options before me. *The Anubis on my left is facing the Anubis on my right. Osiris in front of me is facing the Anubis on the right.*

I studied the images. An answer had to be obvious. Osiris and Anubis were facing each other, and they held an arm out, holding a flail, almost pointing at each other.

*Or, are they pointing to the button*, I thought.

Again, the soft click began. I counted as I searched the area between the two facing gods: Osiris and Anubis.

CLICK.

The wall of Anubis facing me opened.

Fifty-eight. Fifty nine. The light went out above me. In the area behind the opened Anubis door, the newly lighted area waited for me. I entered the opening and started along the narrow passageway. As expected, the door closed behind me.

The passage turned with steps leading upwards as far as I could see.

I started up.

Images and hieroglyphics covered the walls on my ascent. Unsure what the hieroglyphics meant, the images were obvious. It was the mummification aspects. *Makes sense*, I thought. *Anubis was the god of death.*

I reached a small landing with an Egyptian settee. Beyond were more stairs, but they were painted yellow.

I counted the steps on my way. Three hundred and sixty of yellow. Five of red.

I nodded, realizing the old Egyptian calendar was three hundred and sixty days with five epagomenal days. An arched entry led to a room.

I stepped into the room. Two huge oval windows looked out over the mansion grounds. It was then I realized I was in the head of the sphinx. To my right I saw what I didn't want to see.

Gregory Eggers lay on a table. Small canopic jars lined the shelf behind him. There was enough blood to assure me that Gregory wasn't among the living. I nodded, understanding. Those jars held the important organs. Mr. Eggers was in the process of being mummified.

*But, by who?* I wondered.

A soft whoosh sounded. Nothing moved. Absolute silence.

My mind raced through the memories of my Egyptian trip a few years earlier and what I'd learned. Priests did the work and it took two months.

*That's not right*, I thought. *It was seventy days. Who are the priests? This is day one or two of the process,*

It was then I remembered, the butler had exited the sphinx. I nodded. He was my culprit.

*Time to head back to the house and find out what I can*, I thought.

I turned to the exit. There was no exit. I faced a solid wall. I was sure there wasn't a door when I entered the room. I scanned the area. When I stepped up into the room, I was facing the two windows. Turning from the windows to the opposite side of the room, there was no doubt, it was a solid wall.

*No time to panic*, I thought and walked toward the wall. It was smooth. *The Egyptians definitely knew how to conceal openings.*

I played my hands over the wall. Still, nothing revealed itself. I stepped back to review the scene. Two sconces burned brightly. My mind raced to remember them when I entered the room. I'm sure I'd remember open flames of the sconces.

I smiled. When I'd heard the whoosh sound, it didn't register, but the opening to the stairs was closed. The sconces were burning.

I reached up and pulled on a sconce. It seemed too easy.

Nothing happened. The sconce didn't move. I attempted several different directions. Nothing.

I walked to the other sconce and repeated the action. Still nothing.

Once more I stepped back to review the wall: plain, smooth, and unyielding. There was absolutely nothing to direct me to the spring to activate the door.

*Voice activated*, I questioned and shook my head. Too many words and the possibility magnified exponentially when it could be one of the several Egyptian languages, ancient or modern, or English.

*No, there had to be a trip button somewhere*, I thought.

My eyes fell on the small canopic urn sitting at the end of the table near where the door should be. I reached out and lifted the urn. Nothing.

Wait. Nothing happened but the urn had an indent on the bottom. It was a small hex indent. On table a matching hex was visible. I placed the urn on the hex button and turned the urn.

The door opened and the sconces turned off.

I placed the urn back to its original location, matching the slight dust pattern.

My escape hatch was open. I hustled down the steps to the next door. Reversing the actions that allowed me access, I found myself at the entrance area of the sphinx. I found the trip button, pushed, and the door opened and I stepped into the late afternoon sun.

I closed the door and gazed at the mansion in the distance. So many questions, so few answers. Behind me, the pyramid with its soaring walls of glass, stood watching over the sphinx. I placed a hand on the sphinx. With a heavy sigh, I knew, both, answers, and Aswad, awaited me. I started my hike to the mansion.

# CHAPTER FOUR ~ Back to the Mansion

"Did you find what you were looking for, Detective Hargrove?" Aswad greeted me at the door, letting me into the grand foyer.

"Detective Hargrove," Amelia called from the top of the stairs. "Did you find my husband?"

"Let me ask the questions, Mrs. Eggers," I replied.

Turning to face the butler, I startled him with my action.

"What is your name?" I asked.

"My name, sir?" The surprise in his voice was barely hidden. "I've already told you, it is Aswad."

"Yes, but what is your full name."

He nodded. "My name is Aswad Kallis. I have been in the service of Mr. Eggers for near thirty years."

"Can you explain why I saw you leaving the sphinx earlier today?"

"Leaving the sphinx?" he repeated.

"Yes. I was examining the sphinx, walking its perimeter when I saw you leave it. I hid behind the hind leg near the pyramid."

Aswad gazed at Mrs. Eggers, his eyes searching for an answer.

"Answer the man, Aswad," Amelia said. "Explain what you were doing inside the sphinx."

Aswad inhaled deeply. His formal dignity now in shambles, appearing more like a small child caught with his hand in the candy jar.

"I was checking the supplies in Mr. Eggers safe room."

Now I was surprised and hoped my dumb-founded look wasn't obvious.

"Mr. Eggers has a safe inside the sphinx?"

Aswad shook his head. "Not a safe. A safe room. A reinforced room for his safety."

I stood there, my frowning face attempting to make sense of

what I was being told.

"What supplies were you checking?"

"I was verifying expiration dates of the goods stored there. It is part of my duty to make sure the supplies have the longest expiration date as possible."

I gazed into Aswad's eyes. He appeared to be telling the truth.

It was time for me to grab the horns and ride this one.

"I was in the sphinx. I didn't see any storeroom... no, safe room."

Aswad grinned. "You took the passageway to the right and followed it to the dead end?"

I nodded agreement, seeing no reason to let him know what I'd discovered.

"The safe room is immediately to the left," Aswad said. He smirked. "The way you went is designed to distract and confuse. There is a secret passageway beyond, but again, it ends and the person who enters must figure out how to get back to the entrance." The smugness was blatant. "The sphinx's passageways, like those found in the pyramids of Egypt, are designed to trap robbers and lure them away from the true passageways."

"What I don't understand, Aswad." I smiled. "If Mr. Eggers had a safe room in the sphinx, how did he get to it in the open space between the mansion and the sphinx itself?"

Aswad stared down his nose at me, assured in his superiority.

"There is a secret passage between this house and the sphinx. Mr. Eggers is the only person who knew where it is."

"Is it in the basement?" I asked.

Aswad rolled a shoulder. "I don't know, detective. Mr. Eggers never revealed the location of the passageway to me. I was required to use the entrance you know about."

"You have been in the safe room," I stated and he nodded agreement. "So, obviously, you have seen the entrance to the secret passageway."

Aswad grinned. "No. The room, although quite spacious, has never revealed where the secret entrance or exit is located."

"You can interrogate the butler all night if you wish, Detective Hargrove." Amelia remained at the top of the stairs, her hands gripping the railing. "I know my husband. He was like the sphinx, not one willing to give up an answer." She turned to walk the length of the handrail to the stairs. "I knew about the secret passageway, but like everyone else in this house, I have no idea where the entrance is. Only he knew." She drew in a deep breath. "It was his protection."

She gazed out across the foyer to the huge window over the double-door entrance.

"I can see it is getting late." She stood at the top of the stairs. "I would suggest you leave now before the dogs are released."

"I have more questions," I said.

"I am sure you do," Amelia replied. "For your safety, leave now. Return tomorrow and we can continue this discussion." She cocked her head, her long dark hair shifting to one side. "Is that acceptable to you?"

"I will return at ten tomorrow morning," I replied. "I will probably be here most of the day. I want to do some research tonight and then visit the sphinx."

"That will be acceptable, Detective Hargrove," Amelia said. "I will make sure Jin, the chef, prepares a nice meal for lunch. Until tomorrow." She turned and walked the length of the open area of the balcony to her room.

"I will see you out, sir," Aswad said, bowing.

"By the way, Aswad," I asked. "Is that Anubis statue made of real onyx?"

"Only the best from Egypt," Aswad replied. "Mr. Eggers spared no expense to satisfy his wife's desires and Egyptian heritage." He rolled a shoulder. "Of course, Mr. Eggers was of Egyptian and Chinese descent."

I nodded and opened the door of my car.

"Aswad?" I called to him before he disappeared inside. "I noticed a service road near the pyramid. I want to check one more thing before I leave. Mind if I use it?"

"By all means," he replied and swung his arm toward the glass structure. "The gate will automatically open as you approach it when you decide to leave." He gazed at the setting sun. "The dogs will be released very soon. Make your visit short."

"What time do you let the hell-hounds loose?"

He smiled. "Not time, detective. The dog lock is light sensitive." Again, he scanned the sky. "You best be on your way."

He shrugged. "Maybe no more than ten minutes."

I crawled into my car and gunned it toward the pyramid. I wanted to get a shot of the obelisk in front of the sphinx.

Pulling as close to the pyramid as I could, I grabbed my phone. I wanted instant pictures. I didn't have time to wait even an hour for developing of the film in the camera. I opened the door and crawled out, reached back, and snatched the camera from the seat.

*Better to be safe than sorry*, I thought as I ran around the pyramid and to the front of the sphinx.

"What secrets are you going to reveal?" I whispered to the wind as I approached the front of the legs.

There, in the shadows, the obelisk waited. I glanced up at the sphinx's face. Enigmatic as always.

"I'll make you a blathering idiot," I said and smiled, rushing between the two huge paws toward the tablet.

I grabbed the camera and snapped three pictures of the tablet from different directions.

*The shadows might reveal something*, I thought. With that thought, I snapped two more pictures, one low facing up, and one high facing down.

The hard part was finding hand grabs to get me a few feet off the ground.

I repeated the actions with my phone.

Distant barking caught my attention. I dropped to the ground and rushed toward the opening between the front legs. I listened. The dogs didn't sound as if they were on the move. I walked quickly back to my car. As I opened the door, I saw the dogs appear on a distant mound. They were coming my way.

Turning the car around, I raced for the gate.

*If they get loose when the gates open, that will be their problem,* I thought. As I approached, the gates started to slowly open.

A movement in the clustered shadows of trees and bushes caught my attention. I was being watched.

*Aswad, you old devil*, I thought. *You're opening the gate for me. Thanks.*

I gazed in my rear-view mirror. The dogs were in pursuit. Turning, on the home stretch through the gate, I noticed the dogs stop. They were barking, jumping and in a frenzy, but they no longer chased me. There seemed to be an invisible barrier holding them back.

*So much for their escaping the grounds*, I thought and turned my car onto the tree-lined road.

# CHAPTER FIVE ~ Secrets

Handy-Dandy One Hour Photo appeared to be open inside the Handy Dandy Family Pharmacy store.

Chen smiled and politely bowed to me.

"Ah, Mr. Ha-grove, you need pictures. Yes? No?"

"Hi, Chen," I said and nodded my head to him while listening to his pidgin English. "Can I get one hour on this?"

I handed him the canister with the pictures of the sphinx.

"Ah, Mr. Ha-grove." He pointed to the monstrosity behind the counter. "Machine broke maybe. My daughter, Ping, she say it no work. I turn off."

With a grimace and a shoulder roll, I gave a hefty sigh. "I really needed these pictures tonight." I tried not to show my evil side. "That's okay, Chen, I guess I can go to Shing Han's place and see if he can develop these."

"You no go him. He bad. I turn on machine. I make work." He turned to the store's back and yelled Chinese before turning back to me. "I get Ping to develop for you."

Chen grabbed the canister from my hand. "You come back. One hour." He grinned. "Pictures ready."

"Well, I hate to put you to all this work, Chen." I gazed out the door. "I mean, I can go to Shing's place — it's just down the street." I smiled. "No need to turn your machine back on."

A young girl hustled into the room, tossing a dark jacket on a counter. She seemed flustered at my appearance.

Chen glared at her and spoke Chinese. She accepted the film canister, cocking her head to give me another strange glare.

Chen shooed me out the door. "You go. Come back. Ping make pictures."

I stepped out into the early evening light, feeling both gratified and guilty at my actions.

"Now would be a good time to eat," I said to nobody in particular and stared down the street at Chang's restaurant. "Yeah, some Mongolian khorkhog, fried rice..."

It took me a second to realize my feet were already moving toward the restaurant.

Bingwen greeted me as I entered through the big red double doors with the matching golden dragons.

"So good to see you, Detective Hargrove. Working late?" He guided me to a table in the corner, away from the huddled whispers of the other customers.

"Will this work? Anyone to join you?" He looked expectantly at me.

"Nah. I'm alone tonight, Bing... or, at least, I'm not expecting anyone to show."

"Mei will be with you shortly," he said and backed away.

My head jerked up to stare at him.

He smiled. "She's a new waitress. Very nice." He grinned. "Just off the boat, so to speak. Came from Kaili in the Guizhou Province of China."

I nodded. "I'm hoping you have some khorkhog still in the kitchen."

Bingwen smiled and nodded. "For you, always."

I grabbed my camera and pulled up the first of the pictures to start studying. Spreading the fingers apart, I enlarged the image. A hieroglyphic came into focus and I scrutinized the lone figure.

"Mr. Chang say you want khorkhog. Yes?"

Standing before me was a beautiful, young lady. "And you are?"

"My name Mei." She held her pad and pencil. "You want khorkhog."

"Yes." I nodded. "Also, some pork fried rice, two egg rolls, and jasmine tea."

"Hokay," Mei said and walked away.

*Very professional, all business*, I thought. *She's got to lighten up or she won't get very many tips. Of course, that's not my problem.*

Once more I turned my attention to the image: a vulture, owl - it was some type of bird.

*That means to learn or to understand*, I thought. *At least, if I'm correct.*

I flipped to another picture, one from a different angle. Shadows played on the image I'd studied.

Mei placed the teapot down and poured a small cup of jasmine tea. There were three more teacups turned top down. I frowned. *Why? It was just me.*

"Dinner coming," she said and glanced at the picture on my phone. She stiffened, turned, and left.

I decided to look at the hieroglyphic from another angle and brought up another picture. Again, shadows played on the image, but this time slightly different.

They look familiar, I thought.

Mei appeared with a plate holding two egg rolls. I placed the phone to the side. Once more, Mei glanced at the phone. Her hand shook as she placed the plate on the table.

I frowned at her.

"Why you look at death?" she asked. She pointed at the phone. "That symbol for death."

I shook my head and grinned at her. "No, Mei. That's an Egyptian hieroglyphic for learning."

Mei shook her head vehemently. "No, that death." She took her pen and made a few quick strokes. She turned her pad to me. In those few strokes she'd emulated how the shadow appeared. "Death." Mei frowned. "Old Chinese language. Scholar death."

Now I understood why the shadow character looked familiar. They appeared like Chinese characters.

*Who would put Chinese characters on an Egyptian tablet?*

There was no doubt, I was confused and decided to go back to the beginning and put my focus on the Egyptian hieroglyphics. It was difficult, but I slowly pieced some of the images to words:

Learn; 26,000 moons; Revenge; Royalty, Rule

Giving it a loose translation: Let it be known, after twenty-six thousand moons have passed, revenge will rule... or royalty's revenge will rule. I pondered my translation.

It didn't make sense. Of course, the Chinese didn't make sense, either.

"What did you do, Detective Hargrove? Mei is very upset." Bingwen eased into a chair opposite me at the table. He grinned. "She doesn't want to come back to your table."

I frowned. "I didn't say anything." I pushed my camera with

the picture toward him. "She saw this and got upset, something about the shadow being Death in Chinese."

Bingwen picked up the phone and gazed at the photograph. "I agree, it does appear to be a Chinese character, but it's one I'm not all that familiar with."

"She said it was old Chinese," I added.

"Mei knows ancient Chinese?" he asked aloud.

I laughed. "I don't know, Bing. She said it, not me."

Bingwen stood and gazed about the restaurant. He saw Mei, got her attention, and had her come to the table. He held the phone for her to see.

"Is this what upset you, Mei?"

"Yes. It old Chinese. My honorable grandfather taught me." She bowed.

"So, can you read the shadow characters?" I asked.

Mei glanced away. "Yes. Not good."

"Read what you can, Mei," Bingwen coaxed.

"I only read first sentence. No more." She glared at Bingwen. "You fire me, okay." She drew in a deep breath. "Death to all who read this." She shook her head. "I no read more." Mei turned away from the table. "I go get food."

I stared at Bingwen. He stared at me. We were silent.

"Wow," Bingwen finally whispered. "That's a pretty strong first sentence."

I nodded my head in agreement. "Sounds almost like a threat or the start of a curse."

"Here is your khorkhog and fried rice. Do you wish more tea?" Mei placed the food on the table.

"I'm good," I said. "Can I ask a big favor of you, Mei?" Without waiting I continued. "Can you read the next sentence or two, please?"

Mei cast a glance at Bingwen. "I no read. You fire me. No, I quit." She placed her pad and towel on the table beside Bingwen. "I go home, now."

Bingwen grabbed her hand. "Hold it, Mei. I'm not firing you. If you don't want to read it, that's fine. I understand."

I sighed and crunched into an egg roll. "Do you know somebody who will read it for me?" I asked between munches, my hand covering my mouth.

"You no want to know. It not good. Bad."

With my best pleading eye look, I again asked. "If not you, who?"

She shook her head. "I not know." She walked back to the kitchen.

Bingwen smiled. "I could go ask if anyone back in the kitchen knows how to read old Chinese, but I'm sure Mei has already informed them and..." He shook his head in disgust. "I really don't think anyone will be forthcoming. Sorry, Detective Hargrove."

"That's okay," I said between bites of khorkhog. "I think I'll ask Chen over at the Handy Dandy."

Bingwen nodded. "Good choice. He might know it." He stood to leave.

I lifted my cup of jasmine tea. "To learning," I said.

Bingwen flipped over a teacup and poured a cup of tea. "To learning," he replied and lifted his cup.

We drank.

# CHAPTER SIX ~ Developments

I enjoyed my meal, taking a leisurely amount of time to digest and savor the flavors. Yes, I wanted to spend more time evaluating the pictures, but trying to eat with chopsticks and enlarge different sections of the pictures; it was just too much. I put the phone to the side and watched the other patrons in the restaurant. A pleasant pastime I'd learned to help me understand how people tick. I smiled as I remembered watching an old man seemingly leer into a Victoria Secret store; and discovered he was waiting for his wife to come back out with a gift for their granddaughter.

"Excuse me, Detective Hargrove," Bingwen whispered as he approached. "There is a young lady..." He gazed behind him to a distant table. "She would like to join you." He smiled weakly. "She says she has something to discuss with you."

I nodded agreement. She'd come into the restaurant about ten minutes after I'd come in. *Was she following me? She'd been sneaking peeks in my direction all night.*

Bingwen scurried away, returning to her table. She stood and sauntered toward me.

*Who is she?* I appraised her as she approached. *Young. Attractive. Air of confidence. And money.*

There was absolutely no ambiguity to me, the woman oozed cash. She was accustomed to getting what she wanted, when she wanted, and money was not a factor.

"Good evening, Detective Hargrove," she said, pulling the chair opposite me from the table and sitting. "I hoped our paths would cross."

"You have me at a disadvantage," I mumbled. "You know me, but yet, I don't seem to remember having ever meeting you." I smiled. "Your name?"

"My manners," she giggled. "My name is Ione Eggers, daughter of Gregory Eggers... uh, the late Gregory Eggers, I fear."

"Oh, is your father deceased?" I asked, keeping an

unconcerned look.

Ione rolled a shoulder. "I may be slightly premature in my estimate, but I do feel my latest step-mother is involved with his disappearance." She offered a Mon Lisa smile. "Of course, you probably have the answers."

I cocked my head in question.

"Please, Detective Hargrove. You spent the day at the mansion. I don't see my father, but I do keep tabs on him. He disappeared two days ago." She crossed her legs, leaned in over the table, and stared me directly in the eye. "I'm not a fool, so don't under-estimate me."

"Since you seem to want to put your cards on the table," I said and leaned toward her, pushing the limits of personal space between us. "Yes, I was at the mansion this afternoon. I spent time looking at different things, especially the magnificent glass pyramid and the enormous sphinx. What do you know about them?"

"I was taught my mother..." She pursed her lips. "Not my father's current wife, had the pyramid built to house her collection of exotic plants." She flipped over one of the two spare teacups and filled it with jasmine tea. "Truth be told, my grandmother had the pyramid constructed as a park for the public to enjoy." She shrugged. "When she passed, it was closed. The sphinx was the doings of my mother, Unfortunately, my current step-mother and her cronies..." She sipped her tea. "Supposedly the sphinx was designed to be a safe-room for my father in case of an attempt on his life." She shrugged. "I think Amelia has her own plans for the sphinx."

*A lot of teacups being used,* I thought. *Good thing Mei brought four.* Then the word hit me. *Cronies. What cronies?*

"What do you mean by cronies, Miss Eggers?"

"Aswad told me about them one day," she said. "Shortly after the marriage, Amelia started hiring a bunch of staff to handle certain affairs for her. Two of them always travel with her to Egypt each time she goes." Ione got a distant stare. "She is constantly going to Egypt, and she always brings back several crates of items."

I nodded my head. "I noticed the heavy influence of Egypt in and around the house."

"If you ask me, and I know you're not going to ask me, I think Amelia holds some sort of hypnotic power over my father." Ione grimaced. "That's why he allows her full reign with his money."

She frowned. "Or, maybe one of her lackeys threatens him. It doesn't matter, now. He is missing and I can only presume he is dead and not of this world any longer."

"So, if your father is deceased," I started. "You inherit one third of his estate. Is that not correct?"

Again, Ione rolled a shoulder. "Offhand, I'd say about nine point seven billion, give or take a couple million."

I grinned. "And, of course, you are sure that nobody would suspect you being involved? Right?"

"Not any more than my brother, Leonidas, or my two step-mothers, Kandace and Amelia." Ione grinned. "Well, Kandace really hasn't wanted any part of the family since the divorce. So, if my father has been killed, I have no doubt the three of us will be the first suspects." She reached over and grabbed my hand. "I just want to assure you, there are others beyond us." Ione shrugged. "Not everyone liked my father."

"So..."

"I'll leave you to your meal, Detective Hargrove." She stood. "But, first, a tidbit. Rumor has it my father had a step-brother. Now, if you have questions, please call me." She placed a card on the table and slid it toward me. "I'm sure I can get Leo to join us, if you feel it necessary."

I watched her saunter away. She carried her body frame with confidence. She was in control.

*Is she in control?* I silently asked.

Mei shuffled to my table. "I ask honorable forgiveness. Here bill." She placed the tab on the table and bowed. "I no like to read death curse on tablet."

I smiled at her. "Not a problem, Mei." I glanced at the bill, got my wallet out and placed a twenty on the tab. "Keep the change."

She nodded, and smiled at me. "Thank you." She took the tab and bill, turned and walked away.

I headed out the front door. Handy Dandy One Hour Photo waited for me.

Less than ten minutes and I walked into Handy Dandy Family Pharmacy. Chen glanced up from behind the counter.

"Ah, Mr. Ha-grove. You back. Pictures ready." He held up a hand toward the photo counter. "Ping! Bring Mr. Ha-grove his pictures." He turned to me. "It cost six dollars, ninety-five cents." He smiled. "All pictures good." He frowned.

"Did you look at them?" I asked.

"I see. No pay attention." He heaved a sigh. "So many pictures, stop looking at them. Just peek to see if okay and focus."

"Fine," I replied. "I think there are a couple I would like you to see — if you don't mind." I paused to scrutinize the store for customers; it was empty. "I was at Gregory Eggers' place today and took these."

Chen's attitude changed. "He rich man. No honor for family. Selfish."

I was taken off-guard by Chen's sudden change and distaste for my client.

"You don't like Mr. Eggers?"

Chen shrugged. "No matter now."

I frowned. Mentally I questioned what he meant by the remark.

A young Chinese girl strolled toward the counter and handed me a packet with the pictures. She smiled, but her eyes were filled with doubt and questions.

"This my daughter, Ping." Chen nodded to the newcomer. "This Mr. Ha-grove." Chen turned back to me. "She most honorable daughter. She learn old ways."

"Nice to meet you, Ping." I grabbed the packet of pictures and slid them out to view. A quick shuffle and I had an almost identical image as the one on my phone.

"What can you tell me about this?" I handed the picture to Chen.

"Good picture. Nice contrast. Good shadow. Well balanced. It is a—"

"I mean, what do you see? Do you see a Chinese word?" I stabbed my finger at the shadowy image.

Chen scrutinized the picture, holding it tightly between his hands. "Yes, it look like Chinese, but I no understand image of what? Birds?"

Exasperated, I sighed loudly. "Do you know what the Chinese character is?"

"It mean death," Chen said flatly. "It old Chinese word. We no say it today. We use modern Chinese." He rolled a shoulder. "My honorable father..." Chen bowed. "He know. He dead now. Only a few know ancient Chinese." He sighed. "Many young today no want to learn." He pointed above the doorway. "See sword? Very old. It Jian sword. Most honorable sword of China." He smiled. "Family heirloom."

I glanced at the sword hanging above the exit before continuing to shuffle through more of the pictures, finally seeing one with a lot of hieroglyphics and shadowed Chinese.

"Can you translate this?"

Chen gazed at the picture for a few minutes then handed it back. "It say curse... like legend. It promise future revenge of royal line. It say Cleopatra come back." He smiled. "Like I say, curse."

I nodded my head.

*Just what I needed*, I thought. *Now we have a curse and legend. What next?*

Once more taking out my wallet, I handed a ten-dollar bill at Chen. "Keep the change for the translation." I smiled, put my wallet back, slid the photos into their package and headed for the door.

"Mr. Ha-grove," Chen called. "The legend say it happen in twenty-six thousand moons, but it have no begin date."

I stopped at the front door, glanced up at the Jian sword Chen was so proud of, turned and nodded at the old Chinese man.

"Then I will need to figure that out," I said and headed home. I needed to get some sleep.

# CHAPTER SEVEN ~ Mansion Revisit

Another day; another dollar.

I headed to the office. Once more the sun glistened brightly in the clear, blue sky. All seemed perfect with the world. I needed to file the pictures away and check on a couple of other items that had piqued my curiosity before I headed out to the Eggers estate.

Entering the building, as I gazed down the hallway, I realized something was amiss. My office door was ajar. I remembered closing and locking it. This was not a good indication of a great day.

I pushed the door open. The office wasn't empty. Three men moved about the mess. My files were strewn all over — tossed haphazardly everywhere. I immediately recognized one of the men.

"What you doing here, Willie?" I asked my old companion and police partner, Sergeant Williamson.

He gazed at me then glanced at the scene of scattered papers.

"They asked me to tag along since they knew I was your friend." He grinned. "Mighty thin ice we tread on using the term 'friend' between us."

"So?" I waved at the mess.

"It was called in this morning about six a.m." Willie gave me a cold stare. "You know how much I loved being awakened at that hour."

"Why didn't somebody call me?"

Willie shrugged. "I figured the super had done that and you were taking your good time getting here. Sorry."

"We got a couple of different fingerprints from the chair," one of the men stated as he dusted the different items. "Of course, off-hand, I would say the same prints on the file cabinets match the prints on the files and desk."

"Of course they do," I said. "They're probably all mine. I work alone so I do the filing and everything else in this office." I nodded at the chairs in front of my desk. "Yes, you might get different prints from them. And, you should. My clients and visitors sit in those chairs."

"You don't have to get so—" the investigator retorted.

"Jerry, remember, he and I were partners a few years back." Willie attempted to calm the man. "He's an ex-cop and was a fine one, at that."

"From what I can figure out," another man said as he approached. "They were looking for something and apparently didn't find it."

Once more I gazed about my office with my files tossed like confetti. "Yeah, that's what I was thinking, too." I nodded. "You might be right."

I leaned into Willie. "This is what they're hiring for detectives nowadays?"

Willie shrugged and shook his head.

"How'd they get in?" I asked.

"They jimmied the door," Willie said and gave me a dour look before nodding toward the door. "Not the best security door."

"Not mine," I said. "The building super installed that wonder."

Willie grinned. "At least he went big time and bought the twelve-dollar set instead of the three-dollar special." He rolled a shoulder. "A true security system would have been better. Now, as to who did this? This is not the first time this person has broken into a place. Even an amateur would have left signs of being a novice. This person is a professional. Whoever they are, they know how to get in and get out without leaving traces." He glanced at the mess. "They left this mess for us to think it was an amateur."

"I wonder what they wanted?" I asked. "There's not really anything of value in here and... well, my files are limited." I paused. "The only thing not here was these pictures I took yesterday and had developed. I took them home last night rather than coming back here to file them."

"Pictures?" Willie questioned. "Let me see."

I handed him the package and he fanned out the pictures on the desk to view.

"Hieroglyphics?" He stabbed his index finger at one picture. "Somebody wants to steal pictures of hieroglyphics?"

"Maybe they thought I had other pictures," I offered.

"Uh-huh," Willie mumbled. "So, what's this about?"

I grimaced.

"C'mon, Barry. Share," Willie coaxed. "Obviously you have a case. What is it?"

"I was hired by Amelia Eggers to find her husband."

Willie shook his head and cocked a raised eyebrow in my direction. "How do you do it? I get assigned a case, and bam! You're already on the sidelines, waiting."

"What do you mean?" I gave Willie a questioning gaze.

"Leo Eggers filed a report this morning. It was assigned to me, but I had to come to this break-in first."

"Let me guess," I said. "Gregory Eggers is missing."

Willie hung his head and shook, it back and forth. "Again, how do you do it?"

"Simple," I replied. "Amelia hired me two days ago. She felt her husband had been killed or kidnapped and knew she would be the first suspect."

"So, what have you learned so far?" Willie folded his arms across his chest. "We share, remember?"

I glanced down at the pictures strewn across the desk. "For starters, somebody wanted these."

I wanted to spill the beans about the sphinx and the mummification process started on Gregory Eggers, but I couldn't reveal that information. At least, not yet.

"I will be going to visit Amelia today. Want to join me?" I grinned. "You won't believe where I want to take you."

"Take me? Like a date? You bring or send flowers to me at the precinct and I'll have you arrested so fast," Willie said, smiling from ear to ear. "What time?"

"How about an hour, say around nine?" I paused. "I want to get copies of these photos made and I know where I can get it done in record time."

"So, you want me to stay here?" He glanced at his two companions "With Tweedle Dee and Dum?"

I grinned. "Sure. And, if you feel like you need to do something, you can file some of the stuff back in the drawers. I'll be back." I sped out the door and headed for Chen's Handy Dandy.

# # #

"Chen," I called, rushing into the store. He was stocking a shelf. "I need another set of the pictures and I need them really fast. Can you do it in less than an hour?"

"I have pictures almost ready, Mr. Ha-grove" Chen said. "Your assistant ordered them earlier."

"My what?"

"Ping say he little man. He come. He say he your assistant and need copies of pictures from last night." Chen blushed. "I forget to include negatives. I have new picture set made." He nodded at the photo area. "Ping almost done. I give to you. Yes?"

"Most definitely and don't make any more copies unless I..." I pointed at myself. "I specifically ask you." I placed a firm, yet comforting hand on Chen's shoulder. "I don't have an assistant."

Chen's eyes widened. "Oh? I make mistake. Yes?"

"Don't worry about it, Chen. I'll pay for the pictures and when my assistant, as he calls himself, comes in to get them, let him know I picked them up."

"Okay, Mr. Ha-grove."

We strolled to the photo area. Ping was behind the machine neatly packaging the photos. Chen grabbed the extra set of pictures with the negatives and handed them to me. "No charge, Mr. Ha-grove. I make mistake."

Ping frowned then offered a weak smile.

"Thanks, Chen," I replied and slid a ten-spot at him. "Take it, you made my day a little easier."

I walked to the door. Once more I gazed up at the Jian sword, all the while contemplating whether I should wait to see who my mysterious assistant was. I decided against it and left the store. Still, the idea of somebody pretending to be my assistant nagged at me. I wanted to turn around and go back to watch. I noticed Willie standing in front of my building, searching the street.

I waved. He motioned me to him; there was an urgency in his frantic waving.

Picking up my walking speed, I shortened the distance between us.

"What's the problem?" I asked.

"Get in the car, Barry," Willie ordered. "We're on our way to the Eggers mansion."

I frowned. "What happened?"

"Seems we have a murder."

I opened the car door and took a deep breath. I'd hoped Gregory's body would stay hidden a little longer. Still, I was curious as to how it had been discovered.

Getting in the squad car, I told Willie about my so-called assistant. He radioed back to Tweedle Dee and told him to go to Chen's and wait for the assistant. When the person showed, arrest and hold them until his return. Willie turned to me.

"At least, we'll get one of the mysteries answered," he said and pushed the gas pedal to speed up.

# CHAPTER EIGHT ~ The Body

Twenty minutes later, Willie pulled into the driveway and pushed the speaker button.

"May I help you?"

I recognized Aswad's voice.

"Sergeant Williamson with the police. I have with me Barry Hargrove."

"Very well," Aswad's voice droned. "Please pull up to the front door. Park near the statue of Osiris with Anubis at his feet. I'll greet you at the door."

Willie gave me a frowned questioning look. "Osiris? Anubis?"

I smiled. "That's just the tip of the iceberg, Willie. Wait until you see the pyramid and sphinx."

"The what?"

I pointed across the lawn at the glass structure coming into view. "That's the pyramid. The sphinx is just to the left of it. You can just see the top of it from here." I leaned toward him and pointed out the window. "See that tan area? When we get the front door, you'll be able to see it all."

Willie maneuvered the driveway. The mansion loomed ahead.

"There," I said and pointed at the tall statue of Osiris and Anubis. "Genuine onyx on the little guy, so don't hit it. Park just beyond it and we'll walk to the front doors." I grinned and pointed at the floating pagoda. "By the way, when you get a little time, you might want to check it out with a tester."

Willie frowned.

I winked. "You should find a few drops of blood on the left front settee foot."

"Maybe I should go check..."

I grabbed his arm to hold him back. "Hold on, Willie. Right now, you get to see how the other half lives." I hesitated. "A bit too rich for my blood."

"Servants catering to my every whim?" Willie shook his head and laughed aloud. "I could quickly get used to the lifestyle of the rich and famous."

As promised, Aswad stood near the massive doors, waiting for us.

"Good morning, gentlemen," he said with a slight bow. "This way, please. Mrs. Eggers will greet you on the back patio by the gardens and pool." He turned. "Please follow me." He strolled to the great double door entrance. They opened with his gentle push. He once more turned to us. "This way, please." He strolled through the grand foyer of flickering rainbows to a hallway leading to the massive glass wall beyond which led to the outdoor gardens and pool.

Amelia sat under the portico, sipping from a tall ice tea glass. She stood.

"Amelia Eggers," I said. "May I introduce Sergeant Williamson."

The scent of cinnamon and myrrh filled the air. It was laced with the perfume of lilies which bloomed in the urns lining the portico.

"Sorry to meet you on such terms," Willie offered. He frowned. "I'm a little confused. I was told there was a murder. Where is the body?"

"Madam, the coroner has arrived," Aswad announced.

"The body is over there," she pointed near the pool. "My husband is near the blooming roses. The gardener is next to him."

I was perplexed. I didn't see any bodies.

"Come on, Barry," Willie said as he followed the three people from the coroner's office.

As told, on the path, near the blooming roses, the body of Gregory Eggers lay curled in a fetal position. Near him, the body of another lay. I could only assume it to be the gardener. It didn't appear to look like the man I'd seen in the pyramid. I frowned.

*That doesn't look like the man I saw in the pictures inside the house*, I thought. *Is this supposed to be Mr. Eggers? Similar, but not the same. The face is missing, but the body doesn't appear to be that of a man in his sixties. Plus, the Mr. Eggers I'd seen was in the midst of being mummified. This man showed no signs of mummification;*

*he was completely dressed. Who was this person?*

I had to get back into the sphinx to answer all my questions, but how could I do it with Willie and everyone watching.

*Aswad!*

"Tell you what, Willie. I will let you get about your business here. I need to discuss something with Aswad. I'll catch up with you later."

I didn't wait for an answer or Willie to consider joining me. I turned and walked back to the portico and into the house, looking for Aswad. I found him in the main foyer.

"Could you do me a favor?" I asked. "You said you restock the sphinx. Could you show me that room?" I grinned. "Humor me. I want to see if I can figure out the secret entrance between it and the mansion."

"Follow me," he replied and headed out the door.

We strolled across the lawn toward the massive sphinx. I stared at the enigmatic face of the sphinx and how it seemed to be smirking at me — knowing a secret it wasn't going to reveal.

Aswad pushed the trip button and we entered the body of the sphinx. He turned left, flipped a trigger and a door appeared to another room. A large, lavish room. I strolled in. Aswad followed.

"This is the main living area," Aswad said. He nodded to the right. "There is a bedroom that way. Straight ahead is the kitchen and storeroom."

Aswad strutted across the room toward the kitchen.

"This is the storeroom." He opened a door.

The room was massive, easily twenty by twenty with shelves stuffed with goods.

"How long did Mr. Eggers feel he needed to have supplies to last?"

Aswad gazed down his nose at me. "He felt it should last, at minimum, three months." He shrugged. "I believe there is enough here to last six to nine months."

"If you have other things to do, I don't mind if you leave me to wander this maze trying to figure out the secret passageway to the mansion."

"As you wish," Aswad said, turned, and left.

I strolled the living room. Shelves were everywhere and any book could be a trip button, or any ornament could also be one. The full-length mirror caught my attention. I stared at my reflection.

Suddenly I was transported back to Egypt. I visited there years ago and stopped at a local magic shop where the owner claimed to a direct descendant of a scribe during Pharaoh Ramses reign. He claimed to still have the staff which his many times over great-grandfather had confronted Moses with.

I smiled at the memory. He was a good man and I still remember his so-called words of wisdom. He stood before the mirror and said 'What you see is what your mind allows you to see.' I moved the mirror and it revealed a wire holding it on the wall.

*So much for a hidden doorway*, I thought.

Analyzing my reflected image, I reviewed what I saw, taking in the background which most people ignore; they only look at themselves.

Book shelves loomed on each side of me. There was a small open area which held three items: a staff, a boomerang shaped piece, and a framed item.

I turned and walked across the room to the items for closer examination. The staff was approximately six feet in length of hand-honed and polished wood. The slight undulation reminded me of a snake. The boomerang wasn't Australian. It was an Egyptian wand, and if so, it was genuine hippo ivory. The framed item was a blank sheet of papyrus and stylus.

I smiled. *Why does he have these items, and why here?* I thought.

Then I saw it. The Shabti statue. I picked it up from the shelf.

CLICK.

Yet nothing moved.

Without thinking, I placed my hand on the staff. It was loose, but I couldn't lift it from the wall. I wiggled the staff. It gave. I realized the staff would rotate. I turned it to the left.

CLICK.

The mirror moved, casting a reflection across the wall as the hidden door opened.

*The hidden passageway?* I questioned.

I sprinted across the room to the open doorway. A long narrow passageway with limited lighting lured me to enter.

As I expected, the door closed behind me shortly after I'd entered.

*As Caesar said as he crossed the Rubicon River, The die is cast*, I thought. I moved along the passageway. It seemed I was headed in the correct direction of the mansion.

The limited lighting didn't allow for much inspection, but it did reveal I had reached a dead end. I now had to figure out how to open the door. The doorknob was a dead giveaway. I turned it and the door opened to a small three-foot corridor with another solid wall to stump me. I frowned, entered the small opening, and finally pressed my hands against the wall. The door behind me closed. I was in a small coffin if I didn't figure out how to escape. The wall I pushed on gave, spinning on a center axis.

I was in the basement and I saw the trigger mechanism at the top left corner. I walked between the two rows of shelving units. In fact, there were dozens of matching shelves with corridors leading between them to the wall which I'd come through. Well hidden, indeed.

I worked my way up the stairs to the kitchen. I walked to the refrigerator and opened it, hoping to find a bottle of water to drink.

Aswad strode into the kitchen with the Oriental chef.

"Detective Hargrove," Aswad said, giving me a quizzical look. "You startled me. I didn't realize you'd come back. My apologies for not greeting you at the door." He turned to the chef. "This is Chef Jin Zeng."

I nodded to Jin and without saying a word, I opened the bottle and drained it. "I was thirsty," I said, slamming the empty plastic bottle on the cabinet. "My apologies."

*Why tell him?* I thought. *I'd found the hidden passageway. I had two access points.*

Now I just had to get back to the sphinx to see if Gregory Eggers body was still there. I really hadn't planned to be caught in the kitchen.

"I'd best see what is happening in the garden." I nodded to Aswad and made my way to the portico.

"Forgive me," Aswad said and pulled detritus from my shoulder. "Seems you have some cobwebs on your jacket." He raised an eyebrow.

# CHAPTER NINE ~ The Gardener

I sauntered onto the portico. Amelia sat at the table, sipping what appeared to be a tropical drink as she watched the men examine the garden area for clues.

"Any developments?" I asked.

She shrugged. "I don't know." She gazed at me over the top of her sunglasses. "They keep whispering so I can't hear." She pursed her lips, refreshing the lipstick in the process. "I do hope they realize one of the men out there is my husband."

"May I?" I pulled a chair from the table and sat without giving her a chance to respond. "What do you know of the Egyptian magicians?"

"Excuse me?" She placed her tall glass on the table. "What do magicians have to do with this investigation?" She turned to look at the men. "Or what they are doing out there?"

"One of the best trade secrets of a magician is a simple rule." I nonchalantly watched Willie and the other men examine the scene. "Keep the audience entertained with one hand while the other hand sets up the trick." I smiled at her. "It is part of the slight-of-hand."

Amelia frowned, the area between her brows furrowing. "I don't see where this is—"

"Please, humor me." Using my right hand, I traced a figure eight on the table, repeating the pattern.

She watched.

I brought up my left hand, slapping them together, a white carnation appeared between them.

Startled by the sound, she sat back in her chair, and stared at the white carnation which I offered to her. She smiled.

"Very amusing, Detective Hargrove." She took the carnation. "But I don't see the purpose."

"You came to me a few days ago wanting me to find your husband. During that time, I have been flimflammed with all this Egyptian regalia." I scrutinized her. "You knew I was intrigued by such. Why?"

"I have no idea what you're referring to, Detective," she mumbled, her eyes belying the truth she knew.

"You don't seem too concerned about your husband out there." I nodded toward the garden activity. "But what I don't understand is the gardener — why his death?"

Amelia removed her sunglasses. The red eyes revealed she'd been crying. "To answer that, I would think you should check with the men out there examining the scene. I believe they would have your answers." She snapped the sunglasses up and perched them on her face before sipping her tropical drink. "I'm here to answer questions regarding my husband, if there are any."

I shrugged, stood, and left her to sit alone and watch.

### # #

"So, what have you figured out?" I asked Willie.

"Nothing makes sense," he whispered while shifting his gaze to Mrs. Eggers on the portico. "She watches us, but does nothing."

"Not nothing, Willie." I smiled at him. "She is drinking and if I'm not wrong, it's more like a planter's punch type concoction. I could smell the rums, pineapple and orange juice, and see the red of grenadine."

Willie glanced at his watch. "A bit early in the morning, wouldn't you say?"

I grinned. "Welcome to the world of the rich and famous." I nodded at the gardener's body. "How'd he die? Have you figured out who he is?"

"Aswad gave us most of the information. This one's the backyard gardener, identified by a bracelet in his pocket. Name is Jack Hernandez. Single. Died from a single shot. No next of kin... well, none that we've been able to ascertain living in the U.S." Willie shrugged. "He crossed the border five years back, been living here illegally and started work at the mansion last month."

"Okay, big question." I nodded at Eggers' body. "What's the story there?"

"Like the gardener, single shot to the head. Appears he was strolling with Jack and they both got shot and died where they fell. No struggle." Willie shrugged and gazed at the two dead bodies. "I can't really facially identify them. We'll need a ballistics report and an autopsy to confirm what I suspect."

"Suspect?" I raised an eyebrow in question.

"See the gate to the left at the corner of the house?"

I nodded.

"I think that is where the killer had to stand to shoot one of them. The other was killed from a higher location." He gazed at the second story. "But, not that high. That's why I say none of this makes sense. If I didn't know better, I'd swear these two were brought in, already dead, and staged — yet there is nothing to indicate that. No drag marks, dripping blood... in fact, the lack of blood really stumps me."

"How much longer do you think you'll need," I asked.

"I'd say at least another half hour. Why? You got a date?"

"I need to check out something," I said. "I'll be back."

"Wait a minute, Barry. Start sharing. I just gave you more information than I should have. Now it is time for you to share whatever you suspect."

I winked at Willie. "Trust me," I said. "When I get back, I might have more information to confuse you even more." I gazed at Egger's body. "That might not be Mr. Eggers."

Willie frowned. "What do you—"

I hustled into the house, ignoring his words and slipped into the kitchen. Nobody was present. I slipped down the stairs to the basement. Again, nobody. I strolled to the aisle that had the concealed door, touched the trigger button on the wall, and watched as the door rotated on its axis.

There was no handle on the door on this side. I hadn't noticed that when coming out. The trip wall closed, locking me in the small area between the basement and the passageway. My minor case of claustrophobia started to kick in. I took a deep breath. The only logical thing seemed to be push the door. It moved slightly and then it clicked. It was a soft click, yet I could locate the sound and felt the area with my left hand just at my eye level. A lever stood out. I pushed it. The door opened and the lights of the passageway turned on.

I rushed into the hallway, its limited open space freeing my claustrophobia. I moved toward the sphinx and safety room. I tripped the switch and entered. All was silent, I was alone.

*Now, get to the head of the sphinx*, I thought.

I stepped out of the safety room and headed down the opposite corridor, tripping mechanisms as needed. I walked up the final steps to the mummification room.

On the table, Gregory Eggers still awaited future mummification.

Two Gregory Eggers!

I inhaled to clear my head. Logic enveloped me. The man before me was definitely Gregory Eggers. The man in the garden? We had taken Amelia's word for it since facial recognition wasn't easy with the bullet's exit destroying most of it. My mind raced with questions.

*Time to let Willie in on the secret*, I thought. *He isn't going to be happy with the truth.*

I headed back down the sloping hallway and tripped the switches to find myself at the exit on the side of the sphinx. I flicked the button and stepped into the sunshine.

To my right was the glass pyramid. *A huge greenhouse. Why?* I thought and stared at the huge glass structure. Behind me was the sphinx. *Both of them, huge enigmas to be explained.* I turned to look at the sphinx's face. *What is your secret?* I thought.

The sphinx stared at me. Silent.

I folded my arms before me. "Who is your priest?" I mumbled the question while glaring at the sphinx, hoping for an answer.

Silence.

I heaved a sigh. "Best go get Willie and share my secret," I muttered, turned, and headed for the mansion.

Walking beneath the shadow of Osiris, I made my way up the steps to the house.

"Whatever are you doing outside, Detective Hargrove?" Aswad asked as he opened the door for me. I never had a chance to knock.

"I didn't see you leave and go back to the sphinx," he said. There was concern in his voice. "The monitors usually pick up any movement outside and notify me."

He watched me, waiting.

I smiled at him. "Sometimes I'm able to slip under the radar." I rolled a shoulder in a shrug. "Now, I need to speak with Sgt.

Williamson."

"As you wish," Aswad replied, a slight frown as he watched me. "He is still out in the back garden." He motioned me to the hallway which lead through the house and to the portico behind. "I'll have Jin create a treat for you and Sgt. Williamson." He watched me. "Have you ever tasted tiger nut cakes?" Aswad shrugged. " A delicacy in Pharaoh Rekhmire's rule. Mr. Eggers enjoyed them." He grinned. "I think Jin has some. I think you'll like them."

# CHAPTER TEN ~ Two Eggers

Willie looked up as I strode onto the portico. Amelia offered a disinterested glance and continued to sip the drink in hand.

"Finished here?" I asked, noticing the medics putting the body bags onto the gurneys.

"Yeah," Willie mumbled. "Still, something doesn't seem quite right." He frowned and again surveyed the area, taking time to scrutinize the entrance gate and the roof line.

"Tell you what," I started. "I think you need to identify Egger's body."

Willie frowned. "Identify?" He glanced at Amelia sitting at the table. "She said it was her husband."

I winked. "Trust me, Willie. That isn't Gregory Eggers."

"What?"

"Come with me," I offered. "Just follow me. I want to show you something." I headed into the house.

"Can I assist?" Aswad asked.

"Nope," I replied. "I'm taking Sgt. Williamson and show him the safe room in the sphinx."

"The what?" Willie questioned.

"Allow me to join you," Aswad suggested.

"Really, we're quite fine," I said. "No need to bother yourself with this." I nodded back toward the portico and Amelia. "I think she might need another drink. Remember, she lost her husband and I'm pretty sure she is in shock right now." I motioned with my finger in Amelia's direction. "I don't think she should be alone."

Aswad nodded. "Very well, sir. As you suggest." He strode toward the portico.

"Now, this way and make it fast," I whispered to Willie. "We've got to get across the lawn and into the sphinx before anyone else decides they want to join us."

"What's this about a safe room?"

"It appears Gregory Eggers had a safe room created inside

the sphinx. There is a secret passage between the mansion and the sphinx that only he knew."

Willie's eyes narrowed as he stared at me. "Only he knew?"

"From what I can tell, only he had the knowledge... well, until today." I grinned. "Yes, I figured it out. That year I spent in Egypt wasn't a total loss of learning."

"Why didn't we use the secret passage?" Willie asked.

"Because I want to discover who else knows its location." I shrugged. "I'm not buying the story that only he knew of its existence."

"Fine. There's a secret room. Exactly how does this play into the fact that the body I just sent to the coroner's office isn't Gregory Eggers."

"Ah, that's the funny thing about this sphinx. It doesn't say a word, yet it will give up its secrets if you are willing to play the game." I grinned. "Yeah, this sphinx is a real talker."

"Holy crap," Willie exclaimed. "That pyramid is huge. I didn't realize its true size until this very moment." He squinted. "Is that a sixty-foot palm growing inside?"

"Not only a palm, but other even taller and shorter palms, plus several exotic trees and flowers. If we have time, I'll take you inside it, too." I placed my hand on the sphinx, reaching up to trip the trigger lever. "But, first, we go inside here."

Willie's eyes widened in surprise. "In there?" he asked, pointing at the dark opening.

"Follow me, chicken little," I said and ducked inside the sphinx. I quickly triggered the mechanism and the door to the safe room opened. "This is the safe room." I paused. "Okay, it is more like a safe residence. There is a kitchen, storeroom, living space, bedroom, and toilet."

Willie inspected the area. "Nice digs." He nodded. "One could survive an apocalypse inside here quite well." He walked along the wall of wooden shelves. "Books. Liquor. Movies." He picked up a statue. "This is solid gold." Willie turned to me. "Well stocked, indeed. So, where is Eggers?"

"Follow me," I said, and headed for the exit we'd come in. "That's another area of the sphinx."

"Lead on." Willie followed me out of the safe room and back into the corridor.

"We go this way." I led him through the hallways of the sphinx, tripping levers as needed to open doors as we progressed.

"The Egyptians were tricky with all their secret passageways," Willie mumbled as we walked up the last corridor to the mummification room.

"You're going to enjoy this," I said with a grin. "All the answers will be..." I stepped into the room and pointed at the table with Gregory Eggers.

The table was there. It was empty.

Willie walked into the room and gave it a glance. "What am I supposed to see?"

I played my hand over the empty table where mere minutes earlier I'd seen Gregory Eggers. "He was here," I said. "Right here." My fist thumped the table, the white cloth over it muffling the sound.

My mind raced. *How? Who?* I took a deep breath. I riffled my memory, trying to remember all the steps of mummification. *Was the body moved during the process?* I surveyed the area. The canopic jars were still on the shelf behind the table. *They can't bury him without the jars.* I nodded approval at my understanding of the process. *The body has to be somewhere close.*

"You're being silent," Willie said. "I know the wheels of your mind are churning. What are you thinking?" He cocked his head at me. "Share."

"Gregory Eggers was on this table. He was in the process of mummification." I grabbed a jar. "This is one of his internal organs." I held it up so the light shone on it. "This is the liver." I put the canopic jar back on the shelf. "The body can't be buried without these." I turned to Willie. "The next step in the process of mummification takes forty days."

"So, what do they do?" Willie asked. "Store the body in a freezer or something?"

"That's it!" I scanned the walls of the room. The sphinx's window eyes eliminated that wall. *There has to be another secret doorway in this room*, I thought. I stepped back to analyze the possibilities. Logical reasoning led me to the only wall that could have a secret passageway. The wall with the shelf of canopic jars.

The shelf!

I immediately pressed against the wall with the shelf, searching for a trip lever.

A button. There, on the side of the shelf unit. A small, non-descriptive, almost invisible knob. I pressed it. The shelf wall rotated.

"How do you do that?" Willie asked, standing there shaking his head.

"It doesn't matter. Follow me." I entered the new room. "Gregory Eggers, as I promised."

Willie strolled to the body. "If this is Eggers, then who the hell did I send to the coroner for examining?"

"Now you see the dilemma. If this is Gregory Eggers, and if I must say so myself, his facial features match the pictures I've seen, and Amelia says the body in the garden is Gregory Eggers." I paused. "Exactly how many husbands does she have?"

Willie inhaled deeply and grinned. "Like you just said, it doesn't really matter. I have three dead bodies." He gazed at me. "And, no leads." He gazed at the doorway. "All the twists and turns to get up here... I don't think the coroner's gurney will make it."

I shook my head. "You're not taking this body," I said. "At least, not yet. I want to find the killer and who else knows about this chamber and the secret passageway."

Willie cocked an eye in my direction. "Obstructing an investigation?"

"If need be." I rolled a shoulder. "You know the way back in?" I offered a grin. "I'm not going to show you. Amelia Eggers hired me to find her husband. I found him." I nodded at the body. "Now, I need to discover who is did this."

"Uh, that would be my... MY job." Willie folded his arms over his chest and glared at me. "What am I supposed to do?"

I pushed him from the room, tripping the mechanism to close the secret panel door. "Figure out who the dead guy in the garden is. My first question would be to Mrs. Eggers — asking how she knew it was her husband."

Once more I pushed Willie, this time down the passageway from the sphinx's head and headed him toward the body and exit. I smiled. With a little luck, Willie would get confused as to direction and where the secret trip mechanisms were located, or, at least, a few of them.

# CHAPTER ELEVEN ~ Interrogation

Exiting the sphinx, we stepped into the full sunlight. Willie shaded his eyes from the brightness.

"Do you still want to see the inside of the pyramid?"

"Sure." Willie headed toward the door of the pyramid.

The door opened.

"Hola," the gentleman said, poking his head out the opening. "May I be of assistance? Ah, Senor Hargrove. It is good to see you again."

"Hola," I replied. "Mi amigo, Willie, desea ver el invernadero."

"Okay, what's everyone saying?" Willie asked.

"Forgive me," Jose replied. "Mr. Hargrove says you want to see the greenhouse."

Willie shrugged. "Yeah, I guess so. I'm Sgt. Williamson."

"Come," Jose said while holding the door open to the pyramid.

"What is that scent?" Willie lifted his head into the air and sniffed as he entered the pyramid.

I grinned. "Cinnamon and myrrh."

"Very good, Mr. Hargrove." Jose nodded as he led us through the maze of plants in the pyramid.

"Does Mrs. Eggers use any of the different items growing here to make... say, perfume?" I asked.

It was minimal, but a flicker of his raised eyebrow caught my attention.

"You would need to ask her exactly what she does with all the flowers I give her," Jose replied. "I pick them as she desires." He rolled a shoulder. "Sometimes just the buds as they are opening; other times the blooms at their peak."

"I think we have more important questions to ask Mrs. Eggers," Willie offered. "We'd best get back to her. But I do have a question for you, Jose. How well did you know Jack Hernandez?"

"He is a new hire. I believe another on Mrs. Eggers' staff hired him." Jose shrugged. "He did the work assigned and did it well with very little overview. He was a good worker." He frowned. "Why do you ask?"

"He was identified as one of the two dead men found in the pool area garden this morning," Willie said as he opened the door of the pyramid near the sphinx.

"Dead? Jack is dead? He called in asking for the day off. He wanted to check about citizenship."

Aswad stepped out of the sphinx, startling us as well as him.

"May I ask what you were doing?" I asked.

Aswad straightened to full height. "I was looking for Detective Williamson. The others are ready to leave and wished to know if you had any further instructions."

"Thank you," Willie replied. "I'm headed back that way. I'll take care of it immediately."

"How is it we didn't see you enter the sphinx?" I asked.

"For the same reason I didn't see you in the pyramid." He offered a disdainful glance down his sharp nose. "Too much overgrowth." He cast a glance at Jose. "Perhaps you need to attend to your duties as gardener and properly maintain the jungle inside the pyramid." He turned and headed for the main house.

"Guess we follow him," I mumbled to Willie then lowered my voice even more. "Are you going to question Mrs. Eggers?"

Willie nodded. "Something is not adding up," he whispered back. "IF Jack was off today, how did he come up dead in the garden?"

"My hearing is extremely acute, gentlemen," Aswad said while continuing to look forward. "Mrs. Eggers is now in her library if you wish to see her." He stopped and turned to face us. "If things aren't adding up, perhaps I can shed some light on the subject. Ask me questions and I will answer them."

Once more he turned to the mansion and walked.

I had to ask. "Tell me, Aswad. What do you get with the death of Gregory Eggers?"

"Nothing. Not one penny." Once more he turned to face us, a sly grin on his face. "I have nothing to gain with his death. I had no reason to see him dead. I will probably be unemployed shortly." He cocked a questioning eyebrow. "Does that remove me from the list of suspects?" He shrugged. "None of the staff receive any inheritance. We are staff, not family."

"So, who has the most to gain?" Willie asked.

"Only three people, Sgt. Williamson. That would be Amelia Eggers, Ione Eggers, and Leonidas Eggers."

As we approached the kitchen entrance, the sound of wheels grinding on gravel caught my attention.

"Somebody is visiting?" I asked.

"Three of Mrs. Eggers business associates arrived earlier." With a nonchalant roll of the shoulder, he grimaced. "They were in the library. I believe that was the sound of them leaving. She will be upset with me for not being there to see them out."

"You don't seem too concerned, Aswad," I said.

"I am but a mere butler, Mr. Hargrove," Aswad replied. "I can't be everywhere on this estate at the same time." He smiled weakly. "I'm sure they were able to see themselves out."

Aswad opened the kitchen door and allowed us to enter first.

"Mrs. Eggers should still be in her library." He turned to me. "You do remember where it is, yes?"

I nodded.

"Do you need any further assistance?" He stood with his hands folded together and bowed ever-so slightly.

"I'm fine," I said and gazed at Willie who nodded agreement. I escorted Willie toward Amelia's library. Stopping in front of the huge wooden doors, I gently knocked before opening the door.

"Yes?" Amelia said, turning to face us. She held a large scroll between her outstretched hands.

"I have a few questions, Mrs. Eggers," Willie said.

In a dramatic move, Amelia dropped the map from her left hand, using it to reach out and grab the desk to support her. She leaned back in a swoon.

"The day has been exhaustive," she said. "I fear I've not the strength for..." She shook her head. "I mean, the curse is getting harder and harder each time. My lovers, my husbands. She inhaled deeply. "They're gone. Dead. It is a curse."

I frowned at her antics. *Lovers? Husbands? At twenty-five-ish?* My mind raced with thoughts.

"Could we continue this tomorrow?" She gazed off into a corner. "I mean, my husband was killed this morning. I feel I need a little time—"

"I understand, Mrs. Eggers," Willie said. "Still, I need to interview you so I can get a proper investigation started. Can you tell me how it happened?"

Amelia slumped into the chair at the desk. "How did it happen? I don't know. I heard a shot, then another shot. I ran to the portico and saw two dead men. Unsure what to do, I approached them with caution. It was my husband and—"

"Yes," I interrupted. "How did you know it was your husband?" I paused. "I saw the body and wouldn't be able to facially identify the person."

"It had to be my husband. The watch. The ring. The suit. It was the same suit he was wearing at the party the other night."

"Party?" Willie questioned.

"As I explained to Detective Hargrove the other day, my husband was missing. The last time I saw him was about nine-thirty or so that day."

Willie nodded. "So, you basically identified the man because of the watch and ring. What ring?"

Amelia eyes widened in surprise. "It was a royal Egyptian signet ring. It was mine when..." She glanced at the two men.

Willie frowned. "Yours when what?"

Amelia composed herself. "When I left Egypt."

I cringed. *That's a lie*, I thought and narrowed my eyes to scrutinize her closer. Her body language ensured me I was correct.

A knock on the door grabbed our attention. Aswad entered.

"Sgt. Williamson. They are again asking for you out in the garden. Should I reply?"

"I'm coming," Willie said, stood, and strolled to the library entrance. He turned back to me. "I'll return shortly." He grinned. "Don't get too involved."

## CHAPTER TWELVE ~ Signet Ring

"A signet ring," I said moving the conversation in a direction I wanted. "Which Pharaoh's?

With a graceful move, Amelia took a seat at the desk. She felt she was in control. "The signet ring belonged to Ptolemy XIV. A trinket I picked up over the years."

I decided to make myself comfortable and eased into a dynastic Egyptian settee. "Ptolemy XIV? If I remember correctly that was Cleopatra's younger brother. I offered an innocent glance to my hostess. "Am I not correct?" Without giving her a chance to answer, I continued. "Would not his signet ring be extremely similar to the one you're wearing? Is that not Cleopatra's signet ring?"

Amelia played with her ring. She hesitated long enough for me to realize I had her against a wall. She inhaled deeply before responding.

"The signet rings are replicas, Detective Hargrove. That much I can assure you." She played her hand over the desk's top before finally sliding the desk's drawer open.

I nodded my understanding. Still, I gazed at the ring on her finger. It appeared quite authentic.

Amelia slipped a vial of iridescent liquid from the drawer.

"Allow a lady a moment," she said and pulled the stopper from the vial and gently applied a drop of the fragrance to the side of her neck. "There. I feel so much better."

The heady scent hit me: myrrh, cardamom, cinnamon, and... that alluring scent of... I didn't know. What I did know, it dug deep into me, forcing urges I usually kept in control.

"Now, Detective Hargrove," Amelia cooed. "What were you wanting to discuss?" She blinked, her eyelids moving in slow motion, hiding the azure blue-colored eyes only momentarily.

I was hypnotized. I couldn't control the primal sensations in my gut which spread lower, forcing me into a heavy breathing. I was light-headed. At that moment there was only one thing on my mind and I wanted my sexual urges satisfied. Fantasies flooded me.

A knock on the door scattered the whirlwind of fantasies. Again, Aswad entered.

"Perhaps some tea?" he asked as he barged into the room with a tray. "Detective Williamson was asking—"

Amelia was on her feet, her arm stretched out and finger pointing to the door. "Out!!" It was more snarl than demand. Her eyes flared in anger.

Aswad bowed, turned, and left.

My head cleared. The fantasy images in my head dissipated. The moment was gone.

I stared at the desk, wondering exactly what I wanted to do next.

"Let me check on Sgt. Williamson," I said. "He should have been back by now." I stood and headed for the door.

At the door I glanced at Amelia. She sat sulking at the desk, glaring at me.

"I..." With no idea of what to say, I stood there like a schoolboy, unsure.

She smiled.

The change startled me, but I was drawn to her. The dream was back, the fantasies filled my mind. I saw tall palms; exotic scents captured my being. Distant buildings wavered in the waves of heat of the sand at my feet. I wore sandals. The finest pleated linen shendyt wrapped around my waist, held in place by a leather belt adorned in gold and jewels.

Amelia beckoned, calling me to her as she lounged on a chaise. Two servants stood behind her, slowly moving plumed fans above her.

I stumbled a few steps closer.

"Do you like what you see?" she asked. "Does this not please you?"

I stretched out my right hand. The old Bulova watch caught my attention. I frowned.

The apparition disappeared. I was half way between the door and the desk. I shook my head to clear the remaining webs of the dream.

*How?* I thought and narrowed my eyes as I analyzed the events.

"Hey, Barry," Willie called from the doorway. "You coming? I told Aswad I needed you."

I turned. "Yeah." My mind wasn't completely clear, but I had the sense to realize I would be in trouble if I stayed in the library with Amelia.

I stood in the doorway and gave her a glance. I now stared at a lost waif, a little girl who seemed to need help... Yet, those eyes. They beckoned, promising unspoken desires. I hesitated.

"Get a move on," Willie offered and pulled me toward him and the portico.

He leaned in.

"What are we going to do with the body in sphinx?" Willie asked. "I can't ignore it." He shook his head. "You know, my job and all."

"If we disturb it," I whispered. "Whoever is involved will know we're onto them. At the current time, we have the upper hand. We know where the body of the real Gregory Eggers is residing."

Willie inhaled deeply and then pushed the screen open to the portico. "So, we keep up the facade of bungling our way through the case."

I snickered. "I wouldn't call it bungling." I rolled a shoulder. "Call it more like offering enough rope to our perp so he... or she, can hang themselves."

"She?" Willie raised a cocked eyebrow in my direction.

"One thing I've learned in this private detective business, never make assumptions. Everyone is suspect, even the butler."

On cue, Aswad appeared. "Would you like some of that tea, now?" He stood there holding a tray with tall glasses of freshly-made iced-tea. On a small dish were reddish-colored cones.

*That has to be the tiger nut cakes*, I thought.

Aswad glanced at the tray. "The tea was hot when I brought it to the library, but has cooled. I saw no reason to waste it." He placed the tray on the table and stepped back. "So, how goes the investigation?"

"What secrets can you tell me about the sphinx?" I stared at Aswad.

His eyes lowered and a slight grin crossed his lips. "The sphinx never reveals all its secrets, Mr. Hargrove." He stared directly at me. "What secrets of the sphinx have you learned?"

I raised a wagging finger. "Ah...ah...ah," I said. "I asked first."

"Very well." Aswad glanced about the portico. "Shall we sit?"

I nodded approval and the three of us cozied to the chairs about the table with the tea.

"I want you to talk freely, Aswad," I said. "Detective Williamson would appreciate your honesty." I motioned to the tea he'd brought in. "Have some."

"Thank you," Aswad replied and poured himself a glass of tea. He sipped. "Not bad, if I must say so myself. I do know how to make a good tea." He glanced at the two of us. "But you want secrets."

Aswad heaved a heavy sigh and took the time to view the gardens in their splendor. "Pity," he said. "Mr. Gregory was extremely proud of his garden." He turned to us. "You probably didn't realize it, but the head of the sphinx faces toward this garden to oversee it."

"Interesting," I said. "What can you tell me of the obelisk between the outstretched front legs?"

"Ah, the obelisk. A tidbit brought from Egypt by Mrs. Eggers on one of her trips."

"I have these photos," I offered and spread them on the table. "The shadows are Chinese characters."

"Jin!!" Aswad yelled, startling me.

A young Chinese man appeared in the doorway.

"You called, Aswad," he asked.

"Please, Jin," Aswad cooed. "Read these words."

Jin gazed at the pictures. "Ancient Chinese." He frowned. "My girlfriend, she read ancient Chinese. She here now."

He disappeared and quickly returned with a young lady in tow who obviously didn't want to join us.

"These men want you to read ancient Chinse curse," Jin said.

I stared at Ping, surprised to see her.

"Hello, Detective Hargrove," she said.

Jin grabbed the photos and showed them to her.

She closed her eyes, a moment of meditation. A deep breath and Ping opened her eyes to gaze at the pictures. She read.

"A curse. At the appointed time, when the queen is reborn,

death will come to the royal scholar." Jin leaned in and moved the photos, rearranging them while examining the images. "Why are these ancient Chinese characters mere shadows on Egyptian hieroglyphics?" Ping rolled a shoulder. "I no read Egyptian."

"I do," I said then grimaced. "Okay, I understand some of it." I pointed at some of the Egyptian hieroglyphics. "The finger each represent ten thousand, so two fingers equal twenty thousand. Next are the lotus; six of them; so that's another six thousand." I counted. "The next hieroglyphic is a moon. The next two characters represent revenge. The next three with the bird is royalty. And, finally, the last is an arm holding a flail to designate rule." I took a breath. "So, you get 26,000 moons; Revenge; Royalty, and Rule."

Ping nodded her head. "Makes sense. See this?" She pointed at three shadow characters. "Revenge. Sword. Death. I translate loosely 'the sword of death will be used for revenge.'"

She stood and smiled, a satisfied grin, but never looking directly at any one person. "Does this help to understand?" She pointed at the Egyptian I'd translated. "26,000 moons is long time; to know it ends, one must know when starts." She shrugged.

"See this?" I asked and pointed at the top of the obelisk. "This is the signet of Cleopatra. If we use her reign as a date and move the number of moons forward..." I did some quick calculations. "We are talking about this event happening now." I shrugged. "Give or take a few moons to switch from Julian to Gregorian calendar dating." I smiled.

"I go now," Ping said. She squeezed Jin's hand.

"So, what does this all mean?" Willie asked.

# CHAPTER THIRTEEN ~ Interpretations

"You want my opinion?" I watched the group, waiting.

"Whether we want it or not, you're going to tell us," Willie replied. "So, spill. Tell us what you've deduced."

I grinned. "What we have here is a simple open and shut case of schizophrenia." I glanced around to see if Amelia was near. "Somebody thinks she is Cleopatra." The three men stared at me with blank expressions. "Fine. I'm talking about *THAT* Cleopatra; the one who seduced Caesar and Marc Antony." Once more I checked my audience for understanding. "You know, the viper thing." I mocked a quick snake bite and sprawling in my chair in death.

"Yeah," Willie played his hand across his lower face. "Sorry, Barry, but I can't put that into my report. I need facts."

I straightened in my chair. "Facts? You want facts? Here's some. You got two dead bodies at the morgue and you have no idea who they are!"

"Excuse me," Aswad interrupted. "Are you referring to Mr. Eggers and the gardener we discovered this morning?"

"Exactly," I said. "Two dead men, shot from different angles and no facial recognition."

"I identified the body of Mr. Eggers," Aswad said. "I recognized the suit. Mrs. Eggers recognized the watch and ring being worn."

"Ah-ha!" I leaped to my feet. "There's the catch words. Being worn. The men were identified by something other than their face."

Willie eased back in his chair. "If you remember correctly, they..."

Willie's phone rang, interrupting him.

"Excuse me," he said. "It's the morgue."

We listened to the one-sided conversation. Willie finally hung up and glared at me.

"So?" I broke the silence.

Willie sat in his chair, slowly shaking his head back and forth. "I don't know how you do it, but you're right. The two bodies aren't who we thought them to be." He smiled. "Fingerprints identified them as Alexei Skorveski and Donte Salgado, both of them work for Eduardo Arreola. The gun used to shoot them in the back of the head was a Tokarev TT33." He grinned. "An interesting tidbit, especially since the last time we arrested Alexei, that is the gun he was using."

I recognized Arreola. "Isn't he the leverage in Chinatown? Forcing payments for protection?"

Willie nodded. "Somebody pushed back." Once more he eased back into his chair, lifted the tea and sipped, watching. "You want to hear the best part?"

The three of us leaned in to listen.

"They didn't die from the shot to the head." He paused and waited for the words to be comprehended. "They were already dead." Willie smiled. "It feels good to have the upper hand." He paused, again. "They had been stabbed with a sword and according to the coroner, a very sharp sword. Neat and clean." He paused and allowed a small curl to show the edge of his lips. "They'd been dead for a couple of days."

"You didn't see the sword wound?" I asked and paused in thought. "You didn't notice the dried blood?"

Willie shook his head. "Nope and nope." He turned to Aswad. "Did you notice any sword cuts?"

"I didn't," Aswad said and gazed at Jin who also shook his head negatively.

Once more Willie took command. "The reason? Not their clothes. All of this was staged..." He glanced about the garden. "I'm guessing for us."

"Why?" Aswad asked.

"IF that is not Mr. Eggers," Jin started. "Where is Mr. Eggers?"

"Time to put more cards on the table," I said. "But, first, what can you tell me of the night of the party? I am told Mr. Eggers spoke with some Chinese dignitaries. Is that true?"

Jin nodded. "They tried to keep their voices low, but I heard some of what was said during the heated conversation."

"In Chinese, of course," I added.

Jin nodded. "They spoke of inheritance, family, and mother." His eyes widened. "Also, a Jian sword." He rolled a shoulder. "They went outside. Mrs. Eggers watched from the balcony."

"Did you see what happened or hear the conversation?"

Jin hung his head. "I am most ashamed. I stood near the front door to hear their words. Another man joined them. He claimed to be Mr. Eggers brother and showed him a picture." He paused. "I did not see the picture, but the man spoke of it as a Jian sword their mother gave him as proof of his birthright." Jin bit his lower lip. "I was called to the kitchen and did not hear anymore."

"Ah, the Jian sword," Aswad said. "It hung in the gallery for years." He closed his eyes and smiled. "As a boy, I'm told Mr. Eggers would take it down and play with it. One time he lost the emerald gem of the dragon's eye. It hung on the wall for many years before it disappeared one day. I believe Mr. Eggers was in college when it disappeared. Until tonight, I always considered Mr. Eggers had taken the sword to college with him."

"So, what's so great about this Jian sword?" I asked.

Jin's eyes widened. "A Jian sword is steeped in mythology and ancient Chinese history. A Jian sword has an essence that allows it to never age. The sword is as sharp today as the day it was created and honed. It is one of the four major weapons of China."

"Great," Willie exclaimed. "We got a magic sword, two dead thugs, and a dead Mr. Eggers being prepped for mummification."

"What?" Aswad and Jin exclaimed in unison.

I grimaced. "Guess the cat is out of the bag." I sipped some of my tea. "I discovered Mr. Eggers body in the sphinx. It is being processed for mummification."

Aswad frowned. "Who? How?" His eyes darted in thought. "In the sphinx? Where?"

"Is there a way to get to the basement without Mrs. Eggers seeing us?" I asked.

"Follow me," Aswad said and led the group to the end of the patio and into a side room. "This will lead us to the gallery and then to the kitchen," he said. "From the kitchen we can access the basement."

I opened the kitchen's basement door and started down the steps.

"Aswad," a voice squawked over a loudspeaker. "Could you

bring me a honey treat in my library?"

"I'm sorry, Mrs. Eggers," Aswad said, pushing the button on the speaker. "I'm currently in the basement. I will have another bring you some honey treats." He released the button and snapped a small pager from his hip. "Harold. Please take some honey treats to Mrs. Eggers in her library, immediately. I'm in the basement and need to concentrate on what must be done down here."

I raised a questioning eyebrow. "You're busy?"

"You have your secrets; I have mine," he replied and motioned for us to hurry down the steps before Harold came to the kitchen.

Reaching the basement, I strode over to the concealed door. "This way to the sphinx," I said. "Just remember, this was designed as an escape route for one person. Things will get a little tight." I reached up and opened the hidden passageway. "Willie. See this button here? When this door closes, push that button and it will open the next door." I examined the room. "Maybe two of us can squeeze in. Jin and Willie, you follow next."

The door closed. Aswad and I stood in the darkness momentarily and then CLICK, the other door opened and lights turned on.

"Very interesting," Aswad whispered. He stared down the long corridor. "And impressive."

I could hear Willie and Jin in the chamber. There was an edge of panic in their voices.

"Push the button to the left," I yelled.

The door opened. Willie and Jin popped out like dough from a ruptured cannister of biscuits.

"I hope we don't have to do this too many times," Willie whispered to me. "I hate tight places."

"We're good," I whispered back. "Basically, open spaces once we get through this corridor. Remember the safe room? You've been up to the mummification room. So, all is good."

"What I don't understand, Barry, is one simple fact. They mummify him, but what do they do with the mummy? Are they going to bury him in the pyramid somewhere?"

I stumbled, his words catching me off-guard. *Where would they put Eggers when they finished?*

The real question came to mind. *The signet ring.* The dead

body had the signet ring. Amelia Eggers used it to identify the body.

My first hunch was Mrs. Eggers was having her husband mummified, but now, with the signet ring, I was being tossed a wrench and it was headed for the sprockets of my working mind. Signet rings are important. They are not to be bandied about like gaudy jewelry. The ring signified importance.

*Perhaps Amelia was correct when she said it was a replica*, I thought and made a mental note to check Gregory Eggers' body.

# CHAPTER FOURTEEN ~ The Priests

We worked our way to the safe-room and I strolled across to the exit near the sphinx's outside exit.

Jin followed, taking in the wonder of the room.

"I never knew Mr. Eggers had this room," Jin whispered. "It is very nice."

Willie leaned down. "Hang on, Jin. The ride is just beginning." He gazed down at the shorter man. "You ever been to Egypt?"

Jin shook his head. "Never."

"This should prove interesting for you," Willie said. He glanced at Aswad. "You only knew about this room? Is that correct?"

Aswad nodded agreement.

Willie motioned to me to head on out. "Show them what you've learned, Barry."

I opened the door to the open area of the sphinx and turned to Aswad.

"As I understand, you have followed this corridor to the end," I said.

Aswad nodded.

"Actually, it goes much further. Follow me." I strolled the corridor and flipped the first tripping trigger on our way to the embalming room in the head of the sphinx. "We will go down, up, around corners and finally be at our destination."

The three men followed me in silence. As we proceeded up the yellow stairs, Aswad mumbled something.

"Counting the days of the calendar, Aswad?" I asked.

The sounds of chanting caught my attention. I stopped and held my index to my lips to let the others know to keep silent. I placed a finger to my ear.

"I hear it," Willie whispered. "What?"

"It is a funerary chant," Aswad mumbled, his eyes widened.

"Only the priests of Anubis know the words of passage." He leaned against the wall for support. "We are intruding." He stepped back, bumping into Jin. "We must not interfere." He turned. "We must leave."

"Hold it," I said. "You, by your own words, have acknowledged there is a ritual going on for a dead person." I glared at Aswad. "That person is Gregory Eggers. Do you not want to know?"

I never thought I'd see such a frightened look, especially on a person like Aswad who seemed to always be in control.

"They are calling on Inpu... the one you call Anubis to lead the soul to judgment and allow entry to Aaru with Osiris."

I frowned. "I thought mummification to be a seventy-day process."

Aswad smiled, regaining composure. "There are nine separate parts of the body. Each is released at a specified time and all gather together when the body passes over." He shook his head. "It is complicated. The priests are doing what is necessary to keep the body together until the proper time."

Willie stepped forward. "If they plan on moving the body, I need to stop it because I can't have a dead body go missing. I already had a wrong dead body at the morgue."

Once fear had shone in Aswad's eyes, now I saw determination.

I moved forward and took the last five red setes comprising the stairs. The door was closed. I reached up and pushed the trip lever. The door opened.

The chanting stopped immediately.

"Who dares to enter the halls of Anubis? Who befouls the process?"

The head priest wearing a mask head of Anubis turned to face them. He removed the mask.

"How did you get in?" he asked.

"He followed the yellow brick road," Willie said. "Now, step away from the body. You've contaminated the investigation more than I can ever hope to make sense of." He stepped closer to Mr. Eggers' body, hoping the head priest would step back.

The two other priests removed their face masks and watched their leader.

"The process must continue," the man said and remained steadfast in his position.

"These are Mrs. Eggers' companions I spoke of earlier," Aswad whispered.

"They are?" I asked. "It would appear Mrs. Eggers was aware of her husband's demise." I shook my head, disgusted I'd been duped so easily. I turned to Willie. "I'm guessing you will arrest these three and also Mrs. Eggers."

"Let me call this one in," Willie said, lifting his phone to dial. "You may want to go down and greet them at the base of the sphinx, Barry. That way they'll they know how to get up here. I'll tell the coroner we'll bring the body to him outside." He shook his head. "Like I said earlier, there is no way that gurney is coming up here."

"Excuse me, gentlemen," the head priest said. "If we are being arrested, may I and my assistants take a moment to change clothes." He pulled at his tunic. "I really don't think this is appropriate apparel for a jail cell." He motioned to the secret room we'd discovered earlier. "Our street clothes are in there."

"Fine," Willie said. "Make it quick."

"As you wish." He led his two companions into the small room.

I turned to Willie and heard the stone door slide shut.

"Damn!" Willie exclaimed.

"Give me a minute," I yelled and searched for the jar with the key. It was missing. I realized the head priest must have grabbed it when walking by it.

"He took the key," I said. "Give me something to turn this." I attempted to move the stone key the vase would have slipped over.

"Here," Jin said and handed me a pair of metal tongs. "If we apply pressure on the tongs, we should be able to move that."

The door slid open. The room was empty.

My shoulders slumped. I needed to find another exit and something told me it would take time and be difficult to locate. I began my search of the room.

"I better go round up Mrs. Eggers," Willie said. "I'm sure they're going to spill the beans to her and I don't need her disappearing, too."

"Allow me to go with you," Aswad said. "I think I remember most of the door locations."

"Fine," Willie said and headed down the staircase with Aswad in quick pursuit.

"I will stay with you," Jin said. "What are you searching for?"

"Anything that seems to be natural, but still is out of place," I replied.

"Like this statue?" He held it up for me to see.

"That is Osiris," I replied and frowned. "Why would it be here?" I glanced at the table; it had a square key on a revolving disk. I turned Osiris upside down. There was the matching hole. I put it on the key and turned.

Nothing.

I glanced around the room again. Egyptian hieroglyphics were everywhere. Then I saw it. An indentation of Osiris on a small arched area. He stood in a field of reeds. It was Aaru. I grabbed the statue — it was the same size. I slipped it into the indentation.

CLICK.

I rotated Osiris.

Nothing. I rotated Osiris back.

CLICK.

Still nothing happened.

I held the statue of Osiris wondering what to do. My glance fell on the square key. There was the indication of a circle. I put Osiris on the key and rotated it a full turn.

The section of wall with the Osiris indentation slide away.

A ramp led down, but to where? I started down. Jin followed.

"Do you know where this goes?" he asked.

I shook my head. "Nope. So, keep an eye out for anything that might be an exit."

The coolness of the corridor surprised me; the others had been mildly warm.

We were at a landing with three walls.

"Either we find a way out, or we go back up the way we came," I told Jin.

"You will find the exit," he said with an assuring smile.

I analyzed the situation and gazed up the ramp we'd come down. There was a slight angle. We'd moved to the right as we came down. *If there is an exit*, I thought, *it will be on this wall*. I felt around and a stone moved.

A door opened. I stared at the outside world. We were on the opposite side of the sphinx. Yet, something didn't seem right. The image of Osiris and Aaru filled my mind while the image to my left didn't fit properly.

"Hold on, Jin," I said and pulled the little guy back who wanted to escape the sphinx.

I stepped back and stared at the two other walls.

One had the typical Egyptian hieroglyphics. It was the other that caught my attention.

"Jin, do you recognize any of this?"

He stepped closer and studied the image of the stars in the sky over a valley with a glittering river and assorted flowers.

"This not Egyptian," Jin said. "This Chinese. How strange."

I studied the Egyptian wall. High, up in the corners, two squares were out of place.

"What do they say," I asked Jin.

He looked at the characters. "It says 'Heaven Gate,'" Jin said. He frowned. "Again, not Egyptian."

I stretched and pushed the two blocks.

CLICK.

The Chinese image wall rotated on its center axis.

"Do you go in?" Jin asked.

"Not now," I replied. "If you wish to leave the sphinx and go to the main house, you can leave now. I'm going back up to wait for the others to arrive."

"I will go to the house," Jin said. "I no like the sphinx." He left and I closed the door of the sphinx and gazed at the ramp I needed to climb to get back up to the head of the sphinx. I needed to check about the signet ring before Willie returned. Maybe I could even figure out how Gregory Eggers died. Suddenly words I'd heard earlier came flashing back into my memory. I needed to see Ping at the Handy Dandy.

# CHAPTER FIFTEEN ~ Back In The Head of The Sphinx

I stared at the body of Gregory Eggers. The priests had removed most of the wrappings in preparation of new ones. The body was naked and I saw the incisions for the removal of the internal organs.

A slash on the one upper arm caught my attention. This was not something done by the priests for the mummification process. I leaned in for a closer examination. A clean cut. Deep.

*This was done by a sword*, I thought and it confused me. I ran my finger along the wound. *A very clean cut.* Looking at the abdomen, I noticed the puncture. Again, this wasn't done by the priests. I ran my fingers across the cut, and on a whim, stuck my finger into the hole. Again, it was a clean cut and deep. Immediately I twisted the body to see the back. The puncture was completely through the body. I visualized a sword being thrust into Gregory's body, forcing its way to exit on the back of his body. Neat and clean.

I stared at the wound; something niggling my mind. Then I realized the issue. The wound was basically the same size on both sides of the body. Also, it was a straight impact. Most European swords — longsword, broadsword, short sword — were pointed and the blade widened as it approached the hilt. Many swords have a slight curve. This sword had no curvature. I frowned at my assessment.

*He died almost instantly*, I thought and nodded, reassured in my decision.

*The ring*! The light burst within my head at the thought. His fingers were devoid of all jewelry. I glanced up at the canopic jars. What I originally had missed now glistened to grab my attention.

The signet ring lay on the shelf. My hand immediately snatched it.

*If Amelia was telling the truth, this most likely was the real signet ring of Cleopatra's brother.* My mind raced at the idea of holding such an artifact in my fingers. I twisted the ring in the light to see the details.

It was not the signet ring of Ptolemy XIV. I studied the ring, almost dropping it when I realized what I held.

*I'm almost positive this is the signet ring for Marc Antony*, I thought. My hand trembled at the idea I held such an ancient and revered relic. To have this in my possession meant that somebody had found the lost tomb of Cleopatra where it was fabled she and Marc Antony were buried. My thoughts were shattered.

"What you got there, Barry?" Willie asked.

"Uh, just a ring I found on the floor," I lied. "Probably dropped by the priest."

"That's called evidence." Willie motioned for me to hand it over.

"Did you get Amelia Eggers?" I tried to redirect the conversation.

"And two of the bad guys," Willie said with a smile. "The head priest got away but we'll have him within a few hours, I'm sure. They're all being taken to the precinct for questioning."

"Shall we get the coroner up here?" I asked. "We got a direct ramp from the ground to this room." I motioned for Willie to follow me and I showed him the exit I'd discovered. "Plus, at the base, there is a door on the side of the sphinx. Have the coroner come around to the other side. You get him. I'll go down and open the door."

I headed down the ramp, trying not to move too fast, but I wanted to get away before Willie remembered the ring I still held in my fist.

My mind raced with thoughts: *Marc Antony would have worn this ring to his death. Amelia has the ring of Cleopatra. Both appear to be the real thing. What is this fascination Amelia has with Cleopatra? Why would she kill Gregory? What does she gain? If not Amelia — who? And, why?*

"Barry, old boy, you need to get yourself to Chang's restaurant and take the time to sit back and reflect on what you know," I whispered, then grinned. "Or what you think you know."

I didn't know why, but it seemed I always did my best work when I was stuffing my face with Chinese food; especially Mongolian khorkhog.

I opened the secret exit on the sphinx. Willie's dark face smiled at me. Stepping back, I allowed the coroner into the sphinx with his two aides as they pushed the gurney up the ramp to the head of the sphinx.

"This place is awesome," the one assistant whispered. "Did you see the size of that pyramid?"

*Pyramid?* Once more my mind went into overdrive. We were near the back of the sphinx's body and there was yet another secret door that hadn't been opened. I glanced at it and decided now was not the time to search. I'd some back.

"Hey, Willie," I called to the group headed up the ramp. "I'll grab a detective and head on out. If you want, stop by Chang's — that's where I'll be."

Willie waved, acknowledging my words.

With the ring still tightly held in my fist, I stepped out of the sphinx into the fresh air. The base of the pyramid was mere feet away. I turned to survey the hidden exit.

*Do I go back and explore? Or, do I come back? It can't be that large of room considering how close we are to the rear haunches.*

I wavered. There was that furtive urge to find out the secret, yet, there was a certain sense of discretion telling me to hold off.

Chang's restaurant won the battle. I headed toward the mansion. I saw Jin speaking with someone. They went into the mansion. My mind wandered. *I thought Ping had left.*

# # #

"Mr. Hargrove, you come back." Bingwen greeted me at the foyer of the restaurant. "This way." He led me to my favorite table near the kitchen and back door. As customary, I surveyed the customers. One couple stood out.

"Will anyone be joining you? Sergeant Williamson?" he asked. "You want khorkhog, yes?"

I nodded. "Some ginger tea, a pork eggroll, and chopsticks. Shi shi ne."

Bingwen smiled. "Your Chinese is getting better."

He bowed once more and left me, nearly bumping into a young man headed toward me.

"Detective Hargrove." The man held out a hand to shake. "Allow me to introduce myself. The name is Leonidas—"

"Eggers," I said, finishing the sentence. "Son to Gregory Eggers. Have a seat. Your sister, Ione, may join us, if she would like."

He motioned for her to join. She stood and sauntered across the restaurant. The other nine customers watched her. One gentleman, alone at a table, tried not to be obvious in his stare, but his eyes followed her every movement.

"Tell me, Detective. Is it true what my sister has told me?"

"That would depend on what she has said," I replied.

"My father is dead."

"Yes," I admitted and tried not to sound harsh. "My condolences."

"So, she killed him," Ione sneered. "I knew she would try something like that. She couldn't wait to get his money."

I frowned. "That's the part I don't understand," I said. "He bought her anything and everything she wanted. Why would she want to kill him to get one-third of the estate? She had access to all his money while he lived."

Leonidas and Ione stared briefly at each other, realization of the situation coming to fruit.

"Then who killed my father?" Leonidas asked.

"I'm pretty sure he was killed the night of the party." I watched the two who sat opposite me. "Did either of you attend?"

Leonidas shook his head.

"Father didn't invite us," Ione mumbled. "He never invited us to his parties after... after..." She glanced about the room. "When we came to a disagreement about his second wife."

I nodded, remembering the story I'd been told.

"I was told there was a squabble, a small disagreement between some Chinese dignitaries and your father." I rolled a shoulder. "I believe another gentleman was involved outside the mansion then everyone left and your father was not seen again after that."

Li Mei appeared at the table with a tray of food. "You want food here?" She gazed back at the table my guests had been sitting. "Or you want there?"

"If you have no objections," Ione offered. "May we join you?"

"Be my guest," I said. "We can continue our conversation."

Li Mei placed the plates of food on the table.

"Mister Hargrove," Li Mei started. "You have pictures? Mr. Chang say you need translated. If yes, I will translate the ancient Chinese on obelisk."

"That would be nice," I said. "But, I don't need it done now. I was able to get somebody else to translate."

Li Mei nodded and backed away from the table.

Ione frowned and Leonidas sat with a perplexed expression.

"Obelisk? Ancient Chinese?" Leonidas watched Li Mei walk back to the kitchen. "What is she talking about?"

I shrugged.

"My father is dead," Leonidas said. "I demand answers."

"I took pictures of the obelisk between the front paws of the sphinx. The Egyptian hieroglyphics have shadows which are..." I paused, more for effect than anything else. "Would you believe? Ancient Chinese." I smiled, watching my two dinner guests mull this new information over. "Also, both the hieroglyphics and the Chinese both are a warning and curse."

"Why would my father have a curse?" Ione asked.

"From what I understand, the obelisk wasn't of your father's doing. It was placed there by your current step-mother."

"I told you she was up to no good," Leonidas whispered to his sister. "She probably killed our father," he added.

"Actually," I started. "I don't think she killed your father. I think she might have had something to do with his mummification and—"

"His what?" Ione asked. "My father would want to be buried beside his first wife, our mother."

"Family plot?" I asked to see what I might learn.

"Only mother is buried there," Leonidas offered in hushed tones.

"Where are you grandparents buried?" I pressed for an answer.

"To be quite honest, Mr. Hargrove. I have no idea. When I first asked to visit their graves, my father shooed me away and said we would discuss it at a later time." She sighed and placed a small token amount of food on her fork to eat. "He never wanted to discuss it. He said when he died, his will would explain everything."

I nodded. "So, have you seen the will?"

Leonidas munched on his egg roll. "The only thing I know about the will is simple. I get one-third of his estate."

Ione shook her head. "I never saw his will." She nodded at Leonidas. "Like my brother, I only know I'm entitled to one-third of his estate." She glared off into a corner. "She, our step-mother…" The word was slurred. "She will get the last one-third."

I fingered my khorkhog, deciding which piece to eat next. "As I stated before, why would she kill him? She had access to all his money. If she killed him, she then limited her funds to one-third." I rolled a shoulder. "In my book, it doesn't make sense. Why settle for an apple when you have the whole tree available?"

Ione frowned. "Strangely, that makes sense. So, who do you think killed him?"

My answer was placed on hold as I noticed Willie come in the main doors. He looked in my direction and shrugged his shoulders, wondering what to do. I motioned him to the table.

"Sergeant Williamson, please meet Ione and Leonidas Eggers. They are Gregory Egger's children. Have a seat. I was just explaining to them why Amelia Eggers couldn't be the killer."

"That should prove to be an interesting discussion." Willie sat and motioned for a waitress. Li Mei appeared and took his order.

"Since you are his heirs, I feel I can freely discuss my findings. It took forensics a bit of time to figure out how your father died." Willie heaved a deep breath. "He was impaled by a sword."

"A sword?" Leonidas repeated. "You mean like in a duel?"

"Not really." Willie snickered. "Like I said, it took forensics to figure it out. The sword wasn't your typical European version. It was Asian. In fact, it was a Jian sword according to Bill at the lab."

"A what?" I asked.

"A very ancient sword from China. Actually, a sword that is prized by the family and has existed for centuries without losing any of its sharpness. According to legend… now, I looked this up before coming here. The sword is passed down from family member to family member. At least, those who have them and it always is inherited by the eldest son."

I nodded my understanding. Suddenly, the image of the sword over Chen's Handy Dandy store entrance door flashed in my mind. It was a Jian sword and one he was proud of.

*But how?* I thought.

"Oh, to make things interesting." Willie sat there with a Cheshire grin, his eyes alight with the devilment of having me over the barrel. "Remember the two stiffs we thought were Eggers and the gardener?"

"Yeah." I let the word slide from my mouth like a waterfall.

"The sword they were killed with also just happen to be a Jian one, if not the same one."

Ione leaned over the table. "What is going on? What is this talk of a Jian sword?"

"It's quite simple, Miss Eggers," I said. "Whoever killed your father, they had access to a unique sword. That, in and of itself, limits the possibilities of who the murderer is."

"So, you know?" Leonidas asked.

I shrugged. "Not yet, but soon." I turned to Willie who was slurping in a noodle from his shrimp lo mien.

He munched the delicacy before noticing me watching.

"What?"

"We need to cut this meal short," I said. "We have to figure out the curse and who the murderer is." I gobbled the last of my khorkhog down.

Willie motioned me to leave. "Go to your office. I just got my meal and I plan to eat it first." He grinned. "I'm tired of leaving meals half eaten."

"May we join you, Detective Hargrove?" Ione asked. Her eyes pleaded. "Perhaps we can help with the curse; whatever that is."

I nodded and stood, noticing Ione's lips curl with a secretive smile.

"Perhaps I can shed some light about our family tree," she mumbled as I stepped back to allow her to leave before me.

## CHAPTER SIXTEEN ~ The Office

I opened the office door and allowed Ione and Leonidas to enter.

"Have a seat," I offered as I rounded the corner of my desk and slammed into my chair, kicking my feet up onto the desk. My phone rang. I stretched to snatch it.

"Hello. Barry Hargrove Detective Service," I said and listened to a man huff into the phone. I was about to hang up.

"My name is Mitchel Gerlach with Gerlach, Konitzer and Sons. By any chance, do you know the whereabouts of Ione and Leonidas Eggers?"

My stare wandered to the Eggers who sat opposite me as I scribbled the names on a pad.

"They're with me right now in my office," I replied.

"Fine!" Gerlach snapped. "I'll be there in less than ten minutes. I'm on my way out the door now."

The phone line clicked dead.

"Do either of you know a Mitchel Gerlach? Gerlach, Konitzer and Sons?"

"That is my father's attorney," Ione said with a frown. "Why did he call you?"

I shrugged. "Looking for you two." I grimaced. "You're right. Why would he call me? It really doesn't matter; he'll be here in about ten minutes." I folded my hands across my chest. "What do we discuss first?" I glanced back and forth at them. "The curse?"

Leonidas eased back into his chair. "Works for me. Exactly what is the curse?"

I shoved away from the desk, putting my feet down, and opened a desk drawer to pull out a file. I fingered through the pictures. I flipped the one I wanted around so the Eggers siblings could see it.

"This is from the obelisk between the paws of the sphinx," I started. "From what I've been able to tell — the Egyptian translates to "Let it be known, after twenty-six thousand moons have passed, revenge will rule... or royalty's revenge will rule." I moved the picture. "Notice the shadows on the Egyptian hieroglyphics? They're Chinese. And, from what I've learned of ancient Chinese, it's a curse promising future revenge of the royal line claiming Cleopatra's return." I shrugged. "I was able to get Chen where I had these developed to translate the ancient Chinese for me."

Ione frowned. "Chen? Chen at the Handy Dandy Pharmacy?"

I nodded agreement. "Is there a problem?" I wrote Chen's name on my pad for future reference.

Ione shrugged. "I can tell you about that a little later," she said. "Let's get this curse thing figured out."

"The question, as Chen explained, is when this will happen. The last Cleopatra to rule Egypt died August 30 BC." I scribbled numbers on the page. "Working with this number, adding another two thousand years and multiplying by thirteen - the average number of moons per year, I come up with a little over twenty-six thousand moons." I smiled. "Of course, we have to adjust for Julian and Gregorian calendars, but we still have a rough idea of when this will happen."

Leonidas leaned forward. "In other words, you're saying the curse is happening now?"

"If you believe in such things," I said. "I guess so."

Ione's lips curled in a smile. "Leo, dear, remember, our wonderful step-mother thinks she is the reincarnation of Cleopatra." She nodded approval. "It all makes sense now."

I frowned remembering the incident in her library. The image of me in Egyptian garb and the surrounding area being of that region, I shivered and took a deep breath.

Leonidas giggled. "I remember father telling me tales of grandma and how she would call him the little emperor."

Ione joined in the mirth. "Yes, and grandpa used to call him the little pharaoh." Her eyes glazed. "I guess you could say he was considered royalty." She shrugged. "Plus, his wealth would put him in the category of high upper class."

The door opened and a well-dressed gentleman entered, surveying not only the occupants, but also the room.

"Allow me to introduce myself," he said. "The name is Mitchel Gerlach with Gerlach, Konitzer and Sons." He strode into the room. "You are Ione and Leonidas Eggers, I presume?"

They nodded.

"What I have here—" He reached into his briefcase and pulled out two large sealed envelopes. "These are the last wishes of your father, Gregory Eggers."

"His will?" Leonidas asked.

Mitchel shook his head. "I didn't say that. These are his death wishes." He handed an envelope to each sibling.

"Please sign here as receiving these documents for our records."

"What of his will?" I asked as Ione and Leonidas signed the papers. I frowned before continuing. "By the way, how did you know to call me?"

Gerlach smiled. "It is the business of our firm to know things, Detective Hargrove. We knew Mrs. Eggers had retained you to find her husband. And, to answer your first question, the reading will be at the end of the next month." He took the signed documents. "That will be on the twenty-ninth at three in the afternoon at our offices." He nodded at the documents. "Our address is on the envelopes."

"Will our step-mother also receive these instructions?" Ione asked.

"There is an envelope for both Amelia Eggers and Kandace Helm. If you must know, there is also an envelope for the house staff." He turned and headed to the door, turning at the door to once more face Leonidas and Ione. "You have the heartfelt sympathy of all involved at Gerlach, Konitzer and Sons. Until next month." He opened the door and slipped out to disappear down the hallway.

"How strange," Leonidas mumbled. "What do we do next, sis?"

"I would suggest we open the envelopes and see what they say," Ione replied while ripping open the large envelope. She unfolded the pages. "There is a lot of information and details of what is to be done." She sat back in her chair. "Unbelievable."

"What does he mean there is a safe room in the sphinx?" Leonidas asked. "What is this about a secret button behind the mask of Ra?" He paused. "And three? What the hell does three mean?"

"That I can help you with," I said. "I've been inside the sphinx. It is a labyrinth maze of secret rooms, doors and passageways. In fact, there is a secret passageway that leads from the house to the sphinx." I grinned. "I can get you into the safe room."

"Fine," Leonidas said. "Let's go see this place."

"Not so fast." I leaned back in my chair. "I want to know about Chen." I glared at Ione. "You seem to know something I feel I need to know." I shrugged. "Spill it."

Ione grimaced. "I was hoping you'd forget I said that." She gazed at her hands. "I did some research on the family tree. Mother's side was easy to follow and it was a simple process." Ione inhaled deeply. "Now, father's side was a bit more complicated. Again, his Egyptian heritage was fairly simple, but it was the Chinese side." She glanced at Leonidas. "Grandma. There were blanks that needed to be filled in and others that required further clarification."

"Grandma had secrets?" Leonidas whispered.

"Many," Ione said and smiled at her brother. "After an immense amount of research and deep study, I was able to discover our grandmother had a child out of wedlock. The boy was adopted and was none the wiser to his heritage until grandma offered him the family Jian sword as eldest son."

Leonidas frowned. "I always thought father was an only child. Are you sure, Ione?"

Ione nodded. "Very sure. Chen Wei is father's elder half-brother. Grandma donated money to him when he arrived in the United States and that helped him to establish himself. At that time, Chen only knew he had a secret benefactor, nothing more. He opened his business, none the wiser of his true mother. It was not until she gave him the Jian sword that he became suspicious and he, too, started to do research on his heritage. That's how I discovered him."

I sat up and folded my hands on the desk. "So, the incident at the party that night; it was Chen who was wanting your father to acknowledge him." I cocked a glance at Ione. "Correct?"

Ione gazed at her feet and nodded ever so slightly. "Yes, I believe that to be true." She snapped her head back up to glare at me. "But I am confident he is not the one who killed our father."

"If not him, then who?" I asked.

"Yes. Who?" Willie asked as he stepped into the room.

"That I don't know," Ione whispered. "I wish I did, but I don't."

I stood and headed for the sole closet in my office. "So, you finished your meal at Chang's and decided to slum with your old partner. How sweet," I said and pulled a folding chair from the closet.

"Not slum," Willie replied. "We are needed at the mansion. Seems there is a party going on and we weren't invited."

"Crashing the party?" Leonidas asked. "I'm good at that."

"Let's go," Willie said and opened the door. "I don't think we have a lot of time. Aswad said it was urgent."

I locked the office and followed the group.

"My car is just up the street," Ione said. "Leo and I will meet you at the mansion."

"I'll ride with you," I said to Willie then leaned in to whisper. "This way you can fill me in on what's happening."

Willie shook his head. "I don't know why I do this. I shouldn't be sharing all this information with you, and yet, here I am, babbling all the details." He grinned. "Wish I could be a secretive as that stupid sphinx on the mansion grounds."

"So, again, what's happening?"

"Aswad called the precinct to let them know Amelia has started a death procession. They called me and here I am. I gave Aswad a quick call to ascertain a few more details. Seems our young widow has requested a large drape of black be placed over the front mansion's entrance, plus more drapes on the pond's gazebo. Here's the kicker. She has created a path to the pyramid from the mansion and it is lined with torches with black and green ribbons attached."

I frowned.

Willie continued. "I asked Aswad what he thought was happening. Seems she came and demanded the body. The morgue gave it to her. Aswad said she is planning a royal funerary for Mr. Eggers per the laws of ancient Egypt when she was queen."

"Oh, the Cleopatra thing," I mumbled.

We pulled in behind Ione's as she punched in the security codes to open the main gate. We followed her to the main house.

Through the openings of trees and shrubs I could see the entrance. As Willie had stated, a voluminous black fabric wafted in the air above the huge double doors. I could see the gazebo decked in black drapes. Amelia Eggers left no doubt about her actions — she was definitely planning for a burial.

As Willie parked beneath the auspicious gaze of Osiris and

silent stare of Anubis, the double doors opened and a tall man wearing the mask of Anubis appeared. Behind him, men garbed in ancient Egyptian clothing followed. They carried a sarcophagus. Following behind, Amelia kept pace with the group.

Willie stepped from the car. Two more squad cars raced up the long winding road to the house. I smiled; Aswad must have let them in. The group stopped to stare at us, the interlopers. I stepped from the car and heard the chanting, an intonation by the one dressed as Anubis, followed by response of the others.

"Hold it right there," Willie said. "I don't know what you're planning on doing, Mrs. Eggers, but burying your husband isn't going to happen." He pointed at the bearers. "Put the... the..."

"Sarcophagus," I whispered.

"Put the sarcophagus down and step away."

"You have no right to stop us," Amelia screamed. "He is my husband and I will have him buried in a proper manner."

"Actually," Ione said, stepping forward. "According to the instructions given to my brother and I a little earlier today, we, the direct heirs of our father, have the final say on his burial."

Amelia glared at Ione. "Who are you to demand this? You never visited your father. You and your brother only took his money. You have no rights."

"Actually." Leonidas stepped forward. "We have every right. We are the blood relative and—" He waved his large envelope in the air. "According to this, we have final say and the current or previous wives have no input to the burial of Gregory Eggers."

I frowned. I now wanted to know what the lawyer had given the two of them. I was willing to bet a huge sum of money that all the answers were within the pages of those documents.

"If you wish," Ione started. "You may continue your procession to the sphinx, but you will place my father in the safe room." She glared at the group. "Then you all will leave." Ione stood her ground. "Is that satisfactory to your desires, Amelia?"

"I have arranged a place for him in the pyramid," Amelia replied. "We will take my husband there." She motioned for Anubis to begin the trek.

"No, Amelia," Ione stated in a loud voice. "You will do as I say..." She glanced at the gathered police. "Or, they will take you into custody for obstruction."

I tried not to frown, unsure if Willie and his group would do that.

"Fine," Amelia conceded. "We will take him to the safe room." Once more she nodded at the person dressed as Anubis. She glared at Ione, narrowing her eyes. "Then I will call my lawyers."

Ione grinned. "You signed the pre-nup, my dear step-mother. Now you deal with the consequences. There is nothing your lawyers can do about it." Ione folded her arms defiantly across her chest. "You were only concerned with making sure you got a share of the money. How do I know? That information was stated on page one. You shrugged off reading the remainder of the document and signed." She laughed. "You weren't my father's first rodeo."

I turned to Willie, unsure what to do. He shrugged and mouthed the words 'we follow' and fell into step behind Amelia's fan bearer.

I had to hand it to Amelia, she looked every part of Cleopatra from headdress to sandals. Even the black fabric glistened with fine threads of gold and silver. The necklace of turquoise and green emeralds glistened in the sunlight.

I was intrigued by the group. *Who were these men? Were they actual priests of Anubis?* Other than Aswad, Jin, and the gardener, Jose, I hadn't really seen many other men at the mansion. Now, there was ten. I was sure the same thought was going through Willie's mind: *Are these the same thugs we attempted to capture earlier?*

Suddenly my mind jumped in a totally different direction. Mummification. The process took at least seventy days. Less than a week had passed. I felt my forehead furrow in a frown. Exactly what was Amelia up to? Was she attempting to hide the body and we arrived in time to stop it? She had to know that Gregory was being mummified. How? A chill settled over me. I was being played like a chump at a poker table sitting in front of a big mirror for all the other players to see my hand.

It was time to fold.

I turned to Ione. "Would you allow me to see the documents the lawyer gave you?"

She smiled and shrugged as we continued on our way to the sphinx.

"Do you think the killer will be found in the pages?" Ione

asked and handed me the large envelope.

"What are you doing, sis?" Leonidas hissed.

"I'm not sure, Leo, but I feel Detective Hargrove should see what our father has directed us to do with his remains." She gently placed a reassuring hand on her brother's shoulder. "Something tells me he will have the answer we need when we get to the safe room."

Leo rolled a shoulder. "If you say so. I guess it is okay."

Anubis led the group to the area before the great sphinx. We all stared at the obelisk at the end of the opening between the large paws.

"Have your last say, Amelia," Ione said. "When you are finished, we will carry the body to its final resting place in the safe room." Ione glared at her step-mother. "The only ones going into that room will be my brother, me, and Detectives Hargrove and Williamson." Once more she cast a cold stare at her step-mother. "Is that understood?"

Amelia shrugged. "As you wish." She stepped forward, taking an urn from one of the men who'd walked ahead of her. She leaned over the sarcophagus, stretching out her hands in an attempt to embrace the whole thing. "You are my Marc Antony." She opened the urn, reached in and pulled a large writhing snake. "If not this time, then the next," she muttered and hovered the snake close to her.

The snake struck, sinking fangs into her soft flesh.

Amelia threw the snake aside, letting it slither away. Once more she embraced the sarcophagus.

"Let me guess," Willie whispered. "An asp." He pointed at the snake.

"Actually, an Egyptian cobra," I replied. "I'd recommend apprehending it rather than letting it get away."

Willie motioned to two of his men and they proceeded to attempt the snake's capture.

"Once more we are joined in death," Amelia said as she slumped on the sarcophagus. "Another twenty-six thousand moons and we shall be together." She crumpled to the ground, gasping for air.

"What? No curse?" I whispered.

"I fear the curse was fulfilled when Gregory was killed," Amelia whispered. "Who killed him? I didn't." She glanced at Ione and Leonidas. "I loved your father." The words barely a sound on the wind.

Once more a chill ran up my spine, reaching my neck and gripping it with cold fingers. *Amelia was right*, I thought. *Who killed Gregory Eggers?*

"Where do you want this?" An officer stood holding a snake out at full arm's length.

"Put it back in the jar," Willie said.

The young man holding the jar lifted the lid. Another snake head popped up, followed by another. He slammed the lid down, pushing the snakes into the jar. He put the jar down and stepped back. "No thanks," he said. "I was given a costume, told to show up at the Eggers' mansion, play an Egyptian servant, and I'd get paid a hundred bucks. I was given the jar to carry. Nobody said anything about poisonous snakes." He gazed at Amelia. "Or anybody dying."

The rest of the group of men joined the young man. Only three remained; the one who was Anubis and a servant on each side of him.

"Arrest those three," Willie instructed. The police moved in and the three men made no attempt to run. "And, those." He pointed at the actors. "Hold them for questioning." He waved his hand in disgust.

"This was not what I expected," Ione said as she gazed at the sarcophagus holding her father and the limp body of her step-mother.

# CHAPTER SEVENTEEN ~ The Secret

"Okay, we're in the safe room," Ione said and pointed at the mask on the wall. "There's the mask of Ra. Supposedly it will lead us to where we need to go."

We all stared at the mask in the shadows of the corners.

Willie scrutinized the ceiling and the fixtures in it. "Let me shed a little light," Willie said and flipped a switch.

A single beam of light glared at the mask of Ra. The light glistened on the golden mask, sending beams of reflected light in every direction. I stepped over and lifted the mask from the wall. There was no switch, nothing except a single gem in the wall. I pushed the gem. It didn't move.

I stared at the jewel and all the rays of light. They beamed within the room from the facets.

"Hm." Willie looked closer at the switch. "Seems there is a dimmer or something here," he said and moved the dial.

The beam of light tightened from a wide spread to a single narrow beam aimed directly at the jewel. The faceted jewel quit flashing multi-beams and finally settled to one single beam reflected across the room to the opposite wall. It highlighted a sole brick.

"That could be the trip switch," I said while pointing at the brick. I raced over and pressed the brick.

Nothing. It didn't budge.

"Why would Eggers go to the extreme of hiding a trip switch?" I leaned against a cabinet, my hand brushing against a pyramid with a crystal on top as the capstone. "Curious," I said and picked up the pyramid. "This is completely out of context. None of the pyramids had crystal capstones."

I twisted the pyramid in my hand, the crystal gem ejecting beams of light as the faceted stone flashed. On a whim, I held the pyramid up to catch the beam of light from the Ra area.

A single beam bounced about the room as I jiggled the pyramid. Leonidas' words came to me: what does 3 mean? *Could it be this easy?* I thought. I maneuvered the crystal until the beam moved out in the direction of three on a clock. The beam hit a mirror and reflected diagonally across the room to the corner near where Ra's mask had hung.

I went to the wall and searched, running my fingers across the wall. A small toggle clicked and a door slid open to reveal the open area on the other side of the sphinx I'd discovered earlier with the ramp leading to the head.

All of us stood in front of the highly decorated wall of Egyptian and Chinese emblems.

"So, now what do we do?" Ione asked.

I reached up to touch the two Chinese characters in the high corners.

CLICK.

The door slid open on a hinge. It was silent. Steps lead down into the bowels of the earth. The walls glistened with a reflective material to light the way.

A voice rumbled.

This is my final resting place
It is not to be desecrated.
Behold the home of
The living god in death.

"That is father's voice," Leonidas whispered. "Did he consider himself a god?"

We continued down the steps, following the slow curve so we could only see a little way in front of us.

"How does one build something like this and nobody know about it?" I asked as I studied the construction. "This has to have been here for decades."

Ione giggled. "We played here as kids and never knew any of this existed. Remember, grandmother had the pyramid built many years ago." Ione paused. "I think father was a small boy."

"And your mother had the sphinx built. Is that correct?" I asked.

Ione shrugged. "So much of my youth is being shaken right now. I thought she had it built, but it may have been built by grandfather." Ione grimaced. "The pyramid and sphinx have been here all my life."

We turned a sharp corner. Our breath was taken away.

Before us was a huge cavern, but it wasn't empty. Luminous lichen glowed eerily, giving the whole view a surreal look. To the right, there were openings and in them were coffins. Ione stepped over to the closest.

"This is mother," she whispered and gazed at another close by. "This is grandmother."

"So that grave site we've visited over the years is empty?" Leonidas stood wide-eyed gazing at the tombs.

"Look at the ceiling," Willie said, unable to stop gazing at the view above them. "It is the whole universe spread out to see." He pointed. "There's the Big and Little Dippers... and Cassiopeia, Sagittarius." He dropped to his knees and stared in awe. "So much attention to detail."

I gazed out at the open area where a river of silver flowed. I knew it couldn't be molten silver, so it had to be mercury. So much mercury. A few of the statues glistened in the reflective light; while others were dull and deep red. To the left, a group of terra cotta servants waited for a command. In the middle of the cavern, a raised golden dais emblazoned with Egyptian hieroglyphics stood, waiting for the last piece of the puzzle - Gregory Eggers.

"This is your father's resting place," I said, nodding to Ione and Leonidas.

"This!" Aswad let out a gasp of surprise. "This is my father... I mean, it looks like my father, and this other one appears like me." Aswad took a deep breath. "Mr. Eggers had terra cotta replicas made of my father and I to serve him in the afterlife." He paused. "So much honor to be given."

I could see the tear welling in Aswad's eye as he reverently stroked the terra cotta image of his father.

"I guess we should bring your father down here and give him his last rites," I said.

"If you don't mind, Detective Hargrove." Ione stepped closer and wrapped an arm within mine. "I think my brother and I would prefer to do this alone without a lot of people knowing." She gazed at me, her eyes pleading. "You will keep the secret?"

I gazed about the chamber. "This is a big thing to keep a secret," I said.

"Please," Ione implored. "The world doesn't need to know."

"How do you plan to keep this a secret?" I asked.

"With Amelia's death, her one-third could be used to keep the estate, the pyramid and grounds open for the public to enjoy for many years to come. I'm pretty sure there are no heirs to her estate." She smiled. "I will check with Mr. Gerlach about the feasibility."

"We still have one more problem," I stated. My voice cold. "Who killed your father?"

"I... I don't know," she whispered.

"I will check with Chen and see what I can learn." I took her hands into mine. "Remember, if he is your father's half-brother, he might be entitled to some inheritance." I drew in a deep breath. "Are you ready to face that song?"

Ione smiled back. "Let the fat lady begin to sing."

# CHAPTER EIGHTEEN ~ Chen's Handy Dandy

"First thing we do," Willie started. "We grab that sword of Chen's and get it to forensics."

"Looking for blood?" I asked.

"For starters," Willie said as we walked into Chen's Handy Dandy Family Pharmacy. "And more."

I gazed up to see the sword over the door. It wasn't there.

"Ah, Mr. Ha-grove. You come see me? More pictures? Yes? No?"

"Not really, Chen," I said. "I was interested in your sword." I pointed at the empty space.

"Sword gone," Chen said, his eyes wide at the prospect of having it stolen. "Why? Who take it?"

"Can I ask a question or two," Willie questioned. "Do you know Mr. Gregory Eggers?"

Chen's smile and happy demeanor evaporated. "Yes. I know him."

"Did you go to see him the other night? Did you have the Chinese dignitaries have him come to the front door so you could confront him?"

Chen studied the group, calculating his words. "Yes."

"Fine." Willie stepped closer. "May I ask what it was about?"

"Mr. Eggers is my half-brother. We have same mother. By right, she give me Jian sword as elder son." Chen glanced up at the empty space above the front door and frowned. "It gone now."

"Why did you feel it necessary to confront Mr. Eggers about this relationship?" Willie kept a casual air about him.

"We are family. I adopted by family in China. They not my family. I want real family."

"Who else knows about this relationship?" Willie asked.

Chen shook his head negatively. "None. Family secret."

"What of Ping?" I asked, jumping into the questioning.

"She is daughter. She not know. Good daughter."

"Where is she, Chen?" I asked.

Chen smiled. "She working on pictures in back room. Developing."

"Well, Chen," Willie said. "We need to find your sword and then take you down to the station for further questioning. Do you wish to call a lawyer?"

"I find Ping," Chen said. "She call lawyer. I go with you." He turned and headed to a door near the one-hour photo area.

"We're coming, too," I said and urged Willie forward. I couldn't believe his reluctance and I could only guess he figured Chen would stay true to his word.

Chen glanced at the light above the door. It wasn't on. He knocked and opened the door.

Ping knelt on the floor in full Chinese warrior dress. The Jian sword neatly rested before her. The dragon with the missing eye glared from its position.

"It was me, father." Ping hung her head.

"What are you doing, Ping?" Chen frowned, asking and approached his daughter. "What you do?"

"Each month you pay protection money." She stroked the Jian sword. "No more. I kill."

Chen stepped back, shocked. "You what?"

"Forgive me, father. I assassinate Gregory Eggers on night he deny your right as elder brother." She glared at her father. "He shame you."

"He no shame me, Ping" Chen said. "My most honorable mother shame both. She no tell him. He not know. Time. In time he learn to accept older brother. I not wanted money. I want his love. I want family."

"No, father. I shamed you." Ping sighed. "I love Jin Zeng to get access to mansion; even dogs know me. I take away family. Forgive me."

It was at that moment I remembered seeing the shadowy character the day I took the pictures, thinking it was Aswad. It was Ping.

"Ping, you my family." Chen shook his head. "Your mother die six years ago." Tears welled in his eyes. "I try be good father." He heaved a heavy sigh. "I fail."

"I fail you, father," Ping said.

She grabbed the sword, sliding it from its sheath and in a swift move impaled the sword into her stomach. She slumped forward, the Jian sword sticking out her back.

Willie lurched forward. "My God!! Call 9-1-1. Get an ambulance here immediately," he screamed.

Chen moved to Ping and held her in his arms, cradling her with love. "You honored me, my daughter," Chen said. "I am the one who is shamed. I should have forced my half-brother to accept me."

Ping's hand lifted to touch her father's face. She gasped. The last breath left her body as her body went limp. She died.

Tears traced paths down Chen's cheek. "I have no brother. Now, I have no daughter. No family."

I considered Chen's words, realizing Ping had been an only child.

"You still have a niece and nephew," I said. "Ione and Leonidas are aware you are family. When you are ready, I will go with you to talk with them. I am sure they would like to get to know their uncle."

Chen nodded and hugged Ping close to him.

THE END

This page left blank

# Rekhmire's Tiger Nut Cake

**History:** Rekhmire was an ancient Egyptian noble and official who served as Vizier and Governor of the City of Thebes during the reigns of Thutmosis III and Amenhotep II, the 6th and 7th Pharaohs of the 18th dynasty in the 2nd millenniums BCE. It is from the hieroglyphs within Rekhmire's tomb this treat is described.

---

Servings: approximately 20 small cones
Prep Time: 20 minutes
Cook time (plus cooling): 40+ minutes

---

**Ingredients:**

2 cup tiger nuts, raw
1/2 cup honey
1/2 cup olive oil
1 cup dates, chopped (optional)

1. Measure out two cups of tiger nuts. Pour 1 cup of hot water over the nuts and let soak for 20 minutes. Then, drain off the water and use a food processor to grind the nuts into a powder. The nuts are too hard for the food processor to grind without the soaking.
2. Add the tiger nuts, honey, oil, and dates all at once to a pan. Mix constantly on medium heat for two minutes using a wooden spoon. Then, turn the heat to a low simmer, so the honey doesn't burn. Continue mixing for the next ten minutes.
3. Turn off the heat and pour the tiger nut mix onto a ceramic plate. Let it cool for 20 minutes. Form approximately 20 one-inch-diameter balls with your hands. Shape the balls into cones, and stand them straight up.

---

Notes:
Most items can be purchased online at Amazon, WalMart, etc. For a more authentic taste like the Pharaohs of Egypt enjoyed, use Israeli olive oil and Egyptian Sidr honey, although regular olive oil and honey will suffice.

# About the Author

My name is Robert S. Nailor but most people just call me Bob.

I'm retired from the federal government. I was a computer geek and still do some programming yet today. One would think I should have plenty of time to write but I actually seem to have less now. So, to make sure that things work out correctly, I force myself to sit down and write. That doesn't always work. Today, writing is fun and I find it relaxing. I get to visit those fantastic and strange places within my mind and well, if I don't come back right away, there is no longer somebody behind me writing on a pink sheet of paper.

I live with my wife, Violet, in a ranch home snuggled into a small wooded acre in NW Ohio. I was born in Sioux City, Iowa but my parents moved to Ohio in 1953. I have four sons and currently have ten grandchildren - 7 granddaughters and 3 grandsons. Plus, I have great-grandchildren – 2 great-granddaughters and 4 great-grandsons.

My interests are camping (have RV, will travel), gardening, music, cooking and reading. So where do I travel? I've been in 46 of the 50 states and strangely, Hawaii is one of the states I've visited. I have also visited two of our territories - Puerto Rico and the Virgin Islands. Traveling allows me to add the ambiance to my stories and to some of the characters, also. Gardening is a bit gamey since we live in the country and have the wildlife visiting us constantly — deer, rabbits, raccoons, birds, squirrels and many others. So, vegetables don't always make it to harvest but what does is more than tasty. There are flowers, sometimes too many, to keep me busy. Music? I love New Age music and my favorite group is Mannheim Steamroller... and not just because of their fabulous Christmas albums; I was hooked on them before that. I also have created some of my own electronic music which I've been told is pretty good. Should I mention cooking? I love to cook and do gourmet cooking. Having worked with Boy Scouts for several years, I have taught many boys the basics of cooking beyond hotdogs and beans. I have won quite a few contests. As to what I read; well, obviously a lot of science fiction, fantasy and some Christian. Horror, romance, adventure and other genres are also great reads when they catch my attention with an intriguing tag line or cover.

# Bibliography

*Novels*:

**Eternal Blood** ~ a Barry Hargrove detective mystery
**The Secret Voice** ~ Book 1 in the Amish Singer series.
**The New York Voice** ~ Book 2 in the Amish Singer series
**The Amish Voice** ~ Book 3 in the Amish Singer series
**The Emerald** ~ Book 1 in the Shiyula series
**Pangaea, Eden Lost** ~ a Barclay Havens, relic hunter mis-adventure
**Ancient Blood: The Amazon**~ a vampire series, 500 years in waiting
**Three Steps: The Journeys of Ayrold** ~ an Irish fantasy for today
**2012 Timeline Apocalypse** ~ the Mayan calendar comes to an end
**At Death's Door** ~ a collection of "light" horror stories about death

*Coming Soon... At some point in time...*

Dragon Feast ~ another Barry Hargrove mystery
The Vietnam Voice ~ book 4; the Amish Singer saga continues
Circle of Stone ~ when more than one Stonehenge isn't enough
I'htha ~ a Native American vampire/werewolf tale
The Topaz ~ book 2; the Shiyula series

*Anthologies*:

**52 Weeks of Writing Tips** ~ tips to improve one's writing ability
**Telling Tales of Terror** ~ essays on how to write horror and dark fiction
**Mother Goose Is Dead** ~ a collection of favorite fairy tales, fractured
**Dead Set: A Zombie Anthology** ~ a collection of unusual zombie tales
**The Complete Guide to Writing Paranormal-Vol 1** ~ various essays
**Nights of Blood 2** ~ different takes on the vampire story
**Guide to Writing Science Fiction** ~ essays on writing SF

**Firestorm of Dragons** ~ an eclectic collection of dragon stories
**Fantasy Writer's Companion** ~ essays on writing fantasy
**13 Night of Blood** ~ 13 amazing vampire tales
**Spirits of Blue & Gray** ~ a collection of Civil War ghost stories

**PLUS more at www.bobnailor.com**

# Book Three: The Case of Dragon Feast

CHAPTER ONE

"The dragon ate her."

His words were blunt, succinct, and spoken with absolutely no sense or hint of humor.

I observed him, waiting for any crack in that sincere, twenty-something year old face. Nothing. I glanced at the clock; almost 5 p.m. and my stomach was screaming to be fed.

Bang!

I listened to the firework scream toward its zenith.

Pop! Crackle! Sizzle!

I shook my head. Tomorrow would be Lantern Festival. Sure. Why wouldn't somebody start today? I shook my head knowing it would be a night of sporadic fireworks.

I remembered how this whole scene began. I was working on my newspaper crossword. I scowled remembering my word choice - 22 down, desire. I had the word 'like' written and now on 27 across, 5 letters starting with 'l' for 'open soda' didn't make sense. I was staring at my word choices when my office door opened. My stomach had growled, and a young man stood hesitantly, deciding whether to enter or not.

I opened my top desk drawer and slid the folded newspaper into it. Smiling, I motioned for the young man to come forward as I stood.

"Welcome," I said. "The name is Barry Hargrove." I extended my hand to shake.

"You're the detective," he said and moved across the office toward me. "I'm James Zimmer." He stretched out his hand to shake mine.

"So, Mr. Zimmer, exactly what brings you to seek my services?"

I shook his hand; he had a firm grip. "Have a seat." I motioned to the two chairs in front of my desk as I sat.

"Mr. Hargrove..." he started, also sitting.

"Detective Hargrove, please," I corrected with a shrug.

"My girlfriend is missing and I was told you really know your stuff."

I smiled. "Not sure who told you that, but I like to think I can do the job." I leaned over my desk. "How long has she been missing? Did you go to the police? Are you sure she isn't visiting her parents, or avoiding you?"

Zimmer twisted his lips in a sneer. "First, my girlfriend has no parents. They were killed when she was eleven, and she was raised in several foster homes." He shrugged. "She really never had anyone she would call parents. Second, of course I went to the police. They've spent some time on the case but have come up with nothing. It was there I heard your name being bandied about."

I attempted not to react to his last words. I was sure my buddy and ex-partner, Leroy Williamson, would know something. A visit to the precinct was obvious if I took the job for this young man before me.

"Who did you work with at the police station?" I asked.

"Detective Jim Preston." Once again he shrugged. "He didn't really seem to care about whether he found her or not." A grin turned the edges of lips. "When I told him a dragon ate her, well, he snapped the lead on his pencil, cocked an eye toward me, and took a deep breath."

And, this is where we were. I attempted to discern any Tom foolery in him. Still, his expression remained stoic.

I hesitated, but still had to ask. "A dragon ate her?"

Zimmer nodded. "A purple one as I was told. We were here in Chinatown for the celebration of Chinese New Year and she asked me to get something to eat. I left her and when I returned, she was gone. When I asked those standing nearby, they all told me the same thing. The dragon ate her." He sat in the chair, hands clasped, rolling his thumbs around each other. "Yeah, Detective Preston was nice, but I think he thought I was crazy. He told me he'd look into it and let me know."

"You want me to find her, right?" I asked.

"If you would. How much?"

I told him my fees and how it worked. He cringed.

"I'm a college student, detective. I have a little savings that I was going to use for Holly and I to go to Fiji during the summer, but..." His voice trailed away. After a deep sigh he gazed at me. "Of course, no Holly, no vacation. Plus, I'd rather have Holly than a vacation."

Watching him, I could see the anguish, the internal fight over a decision.

"Fine, Detective Hargrove. I'll hire you. May I bring you a check tomorrow morning?"

"That would be fine," I replied and glanced at the clock - five fifteen. I was sure Willie would be headed home to his family and a delicious evening meal. Tomorrow, I thought. Willie will be pleased to see me, I'm sure. I grinned at the irony. If anything, I was the last person he wanted to see.

"Is there something funny?" Zimmer asked, scowling at me.

"No," I replied. "I plan to go to the precinct tomorrow morning and my ex-partner who happens to work Missing Persons will be less than pleased to see my mug so early."

Zimmer nodded. "What else do you need to know."

I took out my notebook. "We have a few standard questions. Your girlfriend's full name?"

"Holly Brockwood."

"Do you have a picture of her I could have?"

Zimmer reached into his hip pocket and pulled out his wallet.

"Here's one of us at the park. Will it be okay?"

I glanced at the picture - a little hazy, but I would be able to recognize Holly if I found her.

"It's fine. May I keep this?"

He nodded approval and I placed it to the side.

"Now, her address?"

"She lives on campus in the Kappa Kappa Gamma house."

"Do you know where she is from... what she calls home?"

"Someplace near Toledo, Ohio. I think the town name starts with a 'D' like 'Def' or "Del' - I'm not sure."

"How old is she?"

"Same as me, twenty."

I grinned. "So I could assume she wouldn't be out bar hopping."

Zimmer's face paled. "No. She is very religious and doesn't drink or smoke." He paused. "And, no, we don't do drugs, either." A slight hint of pink colored his cheeks. "Neither of us have had sex, in case you need to know that. We're both virgins and want to be so when we marry."

Without thinking, I nodded, yet, my mind flashed with the idea, if nothing else, that particular point could be in her favor as a deterrent. "Can you tell me a little about how she disappeared? I mean, beyond the dragon ate her." I decided there was no reason to upset the young man with the possibility currently running rampant in my mind.

"From what I could tell when I was talking with the bystanders, the dragon head was the largest they'd ever seen, and the body was larger, covering the dancers. As the one old man said, it was like the dancing lion, but bigger, and a dragon."

Again, I nodded.

"Oh, they said the dragon licked her face with its tongue, then lifted up, opened its mouth, and engulfed her. She was inside the dragon's mouth and disappeared."

I tried to envision the size of the dragon head that could hold a person as described and the men - it had to be men - who could manipulate her into the dragon.

"They said," Zimmer continued. "She probably would be passed from person to person and then released on down the street."

Again, he paused. "I walked the street. I waited in the car hoping Holly would show up. She didn't." He sighed. "I waited two hours after the festivities ended." He shook his head. "I went to the police the next day. They told me to wait three days. So, I did and then talked to Preston." Again, he sighed.

"That was over two weeks ago. Nothing."

"Fine," I said. "You can bring me the check tomorrow. I'll take the case. Meet me here about eleven; I should be back from the precinct by then."

I watched him, unsure if he was in or out.

"I'll be here and if you're not, I'll wait," Zimmer said.

We shook hands and he left.

I watched him exit the door, my stomach growled. I knew I had to get to Chang's restaurant and hoped Bingwen had improved on making his father's specialty - khorkhog, assuming there'd be any left at this hour.

Not wanting to waste anymore time, I grabbed my notepad and the picture of Holly. Once more my stomach growled. I couldn't wait to walk through those big red doors with the matching golden dragons. I grinned. How appropriate, I thought.

www.ingramcontent.com/pod-product-compliance
Lightning Source LLC
Chambersburg PA
CBHW020617130626
46552CB00003B/1018